13/9/24

KV-395-719

SNOWBOUND

SNOWBOUND

Marlene E. McFadden

Chivers Press • G.K. Hall & Co.
Bath, England   Waterville, Maine USA

This Large Print edition is published by Chivers Press, England, and by G.K. Hall & Co., USA.

Published in 2001 in the U.K. by arrangement with the author.

Published in 2001 in the U.S. by arrangement with Marlene E. McFadden.

U.K. Hardcover   ISBN 0-7540-4645-1   (Chivers Large Print)
U.K. Softcover   ISBN 0-7540-4646-X   (Camden Large Print)
U.S. Softcover   ISBN 0-7838-9553-4   (Nightingale Series Edition)

The text of this Large Print edition is unabridged.
Other aspects of the book may vary from the original edition.

Set in 16 pt. New Times Roman.

Printed in Great Britain on acid-free paper.

British Library Cataloguing in Publication Data available

Library of Congress Cataloging-in-Publication Data

McFadden, Marlene E. (Marlene Elizabeth), 1937–
    Snowbound / Marlene E. McFadden.
        p. cm.
    ISBN 0-7838-9553-4 (lg. print : sc : alk. paper)
    1. Amnesia—Fiction. 2. Large type books. I. Title.
PR6063.C43 S66 2001
823'.914—dc21   2001039164

CHAPTER ONE

Even before she opened her eyes she was aware that her body was hurting, her legs, her neck, her chest, her head, especially her head. It throbbed and pulsed with relentless monotony. She was also aware of murmuring voices somewhere above her.

'I think she's coming round again.'

'Yes, she is. She's moving her head. Her eyes are opening. Oh, I hope she doesn't pass out again.'

Cool fingers took hold of her wrist. The first speaker, a man, spoke again.

'Her pulse is steady. Her blood pressure's being maintained. We can only hope for the best.'

Then the other person, female this time, spoke in an anxious, strained voice.

'But what if she still doesn't know who I am? What shall I do if she's frightened again like she was before?'

'Don't worry. These things take time. She took a very nasty blow to the head, you know. Temporary amnesia's not uncommon in such cases. Just be grateful she has no real injuries. Like yourself, Gillian was extremely fortunate. Only cuts and bruises.'

'I know, I know. It was a miracle. The car was a write-off.'

There was a pause in the conversation. She made a determined effort to open her eyes. The light was crippling, bright and penetrating. Then the faces of the two people bending over her seemed to swim into view. The man wore a white jacket. He had grey hair, a narrow face and kind eyes. He was smiling.

'Well, hello again,' he said.

The other person was a young woman with short, cropped dark brown hair and the most enormous dark eyes she had ever seen, eyes that were scared. She had never seen either of them before in her life.

'What's happened? Where am I?'

To her own ears her voice sounded hoarse, rasping. Her throat ached.

'You're in hospital. You were in a car accident,' the man said slowly, patiently. 'Don't you remember?'

'No, no, I don't remember. When was I in an accident?'

Who was the girl? She had sat down now on the edge of the bed and was reaching out her hand.

'Gillian, it happened three days ago. We were coming back from Cheltenham. We'd been to the Everyman Theatre. It had started to snow unexpectedly and was coming down very heavily. We skidded and ran into a tree. You were knocked out, but thank goodness neither of us was badly hurt in any other way.'

The girl gave a faint, trembling smile.

'No broken bones or anything like that.'

'Who are you?'

The girl didn't reply. Her eyes filled with tears and she turned her head towards the man standing by the bed, a man who could only be a doctor.

'She doesn't remember me,' the girl sobbed. 'Oh, Doctor Morgan, she doesn't know who I am.'

'Please, don't upset yourself, Carol,' the doctor said. Then, 'Gillian, this is Carol, your sister.'

'My sister?'

Oh, what was wrong with her? The pain in her head was so awful and she couldn't form any coherent thoughts. She tried desperately to think but it didn't do any good. She couldn't remember being in an accident. She couldn't remember her sister and, oh, no, she couldn't even remember who she was! What was her name? Think, think, she urged herself but it didn't do any good. Her mind was a complete blank. She started to cry.

'I'm sorry I can't remember anything,' she said. 'Not my sister, not myself, nothing. Oh, what's happening to me?'

The doctor sat on the bed and patted her hand gently.

'You've got to give yourself time, Gillian,' he said. 'These things won't be rushed. You've been drifting in and out of consciousness since

3

you were brought in here. You did come round for a short while yesterday and seemed quite coherent but you didn't know then who you were or anything that had happened to you either. But, please, don't be upset, you need to be strong.'

He smiled.

'You'll be able to go home, of course, as soon as we're satisfied there's nothing physically wrong with you. Carol will be with you. She's been sleeping here, hardly left your side.'

Once again Gillian glanced at the strange, young girl.

'Carol?' she repeated.

'Yes, darling, I'm here.'

Her fingers were caught hold of in a hand that felt icy cold and the girl's free hand smoothed back Gillian's damp, untidy hair.

'We'll go home. You'll be all right. I'm home for good now, you know. No more wandering off for me. You're going to get well, I promise you.'

She sounded optimistic, happy, relieved. Gillian wanted to believe her, but how could she when she couldn't remember who she was? When she could only take the girl's and the doctor's word that her own name was Gillian?

*   *   *

Carol took Gillian's arm and led her carefully

4

across the hospital carpark.

'I've hired a car through the insurers,' she said trying to sound cheerful, 'until you can buy another one. Luckily I still have my driving licence though no wheels of my own, I'm afraid.'

Gillian glanced at her. She felt slightly faint and nauseous now that she had left the comparatively safe haven of the hospital room for the outside world again. There was still snow on the ground, though not much. The date was Thursday, February twenty-second. Gillian had found that out by looking at a calendar in the hospital dayroom. It was a crisp, bright day, cold but pleasant, if anything could be pleasant, that is, when she could not even remember her own sister or where they lived or what she did for a living.

'I'm sorry for all the trouble I'm causing,' Gillian said.

She couldn't yet bring herself to say her sister's name. It just didn't feel right. Carol squeezed her arm.

'Don't be silly. You aren't causing any trouble,' she said.

The car was a blue one, almost new. Carol unlocked the door and put the small suitcase in the boot.

'It won't take us long to reach home,' she said cheerfully. 'We live in Bourton-on-the-Water.'

The name was familiar. So they lived in the

5

Cotswolds. Well, she wasn't entirely stupid then was she if she could figure that out. Sudden tears came to her eyes and she dashed them away with the back of her hand. Carol saw the gesture and put an arm around Gillian's shoulders.

'Don't cry, please,' she begged. 'I know it's awful for you but . . .'

'If only I could at least remember you,' Gillian sobbed.

Carol removed her arm from Gillian's shoulders and put the key in the ignition.

'When we get back to the house perhaps things might get easier,' she said quietly. 'Dr Morgan said familiar surroundings, getting back to a normal everyday life can sometimes do the trick.'

'I know he did,' Gillian said in a resigned voice. 'I only hope he's right.'

'He does know what he's talking about, you know, love,' Carol went on. 'He's seen cases like yours before.'

'Oh, so I'm a case now, am I?'

To her own surprise Gillian spoke the words lightly. Carol gave her a tentative look then smiled slowly.

'I believe he also said a sense of humour would come in mighty handy,' she said.

'I'm sorry if I sound so vague, Carol.'

The name seemed to come easily at last and Gillian began to feel more relaxed. Perhaps the doctor was right. Gillian knew she had to believe that he was. She had to believe her memory would return. She was certainly going to do everything she possibly could to help it along.

'Don't worry about it,' Carol said.

It was quite true. Driving along the country roads towards Bourton-on-the-Water, Gillian had a very strong feeling that she had travelled these same roads many times before. And she must have, of course. It felt like a strange case of déjà vu, familiar yet unknown. The snow gave everything a Christmas-card prettiness. The houses they passed were all built of the same mellow, Cotswold stone. They went through small villages with squares and ancient churches. Carol was a very good driver.

'Was I driving or were you the night we crashed?' Gillian forced herself to ask.

She was going to ask as many questions as she could to try to piece together what had happened that fateful day and also, of course, what had gone before it.

'You were. It was your car, but you didn't do anything wrong, Gillian. I won't have you thinking that. The snow had come from nowhere and it was pretty horrendous. Normally I don't suppose we'd have been mad enough to be out in it, but we didn't have any choice. By the time we left the theatre in Cheltenham it was set in for the night.'

'Was anyone else involved?'

'No. We skidded and ran into a tree. You

7

were out cold but I wasn't. I cut my face. Here, see.'

She pointed to the faint but definite scar on her forehead. Funny, Gillian had not noticed it before.

'I was badly bruised where it doesn't show and now I'm various shades of blue and yellow, but nothing worse than that.'

'I've got my own share of bruises and bumps, too,' Gillian said. 'I suppose it was the bang on the head that gave me amnesia.'

'So it would seem.'

'Well, here we are.'

Gillian leaned forward slightly as the car approached the outskirts of yet another attractive Cotswold village. Carol looked surprised.

'Yes, that's right, this is Bourton.'

Realising she had recognised her home village Gillian felt a surge of eagerness and hope.

'Oh, Carol,' she cried. 'I knew this was where I lived. Isn't that something?'

'Fantastic!' Carol agreed.

'Now I only have to remember you and myself and what I do for a living and I've cracked it.'

It all sounded so simple.

CHAPTER TWO

Their home was a bungalow on Bow Lane on the outskirts of the village. Across the road were fields and in the distance the gently-rolling Cotswold hills now with their light covering of snow. It was the middle of the afternoon and the pale, wintry sun was already low in the sky. Soon it would be dark.

Carol drove the car through the open gateway and on to the shingle parking area in front of the bungalow. Gillian looked at the house. At the side of the door was a name plate—Apple Tree Cottage. A pretty name for a bungalow. Presumably, Gillian thought, there must be an apple tree somewhere near, perhaps in the rear garden which, as she climbed out of the car, she could see beyond the garage at the side of the house.

'So this is home, sweet home,' she said, wishing it seemed more familiar.

Yet oddly, she felt that the house welcomed her, that once she was inside it would be warm, comforting, safe.

'For the past two years,' Carol said, going and fitting a key in the front door. 'You moved here when I was living in Rumania.'

Gillian shot her sister a surprised glance.

'Living where?'

'I was a voluntary worker there for some

time, working with a small charity. But I'm home for good now. I'm going to look after you.'

'You'd think I'd be able to remember something like that, wouldn't you?' Gillian said in a sad voice. 'You working abroad, I mean.'

Carol grinned.

'Don't worry. It'll come back to you. Everything will. The doctor was convinced your amnesia was only temporary and I have no reason to doubt his word.'

She caught hold of Gillian's arm.

'Come on, let's get in out of the cold. The central heating's on and I came back this morning to light the fire.'

Gillian followed Carol into a wide entrance hall. She felt a strong urge to look into every room and, without another word, she walked past her sister and opened each of the cream-painted doors in turn. The first, on her right, was a large, square bedroom, with a pine bed and furniture, pink and white duvet and pillows on the bed, draped curtains at the long window. A furry brown teddy-bear, old and obviously much cuddled, sat on the bed.

'That's your room, Gillian,' Carol said softly from behind her.

Gillian walked across the hall, leaving the bedroom door open. The room opposite turned out to be the kitchen, bright and spacious with every modern appliance. Next to the kitchen was the bathroom and the two rooms at the far end of the hall turned out to be another bedroom, rather untidy and obviously Carol's, and the other the living-room which overlooked the large rear garden. And, yes, there were the apple trees that gave the bungalow its name. The garden was surrounded by high pine-lap fencing on two sides and tall bushes and trees at the far end.

In the fireplace in the living-room a log fire was crackling merrily, protected by a sturdy fireguard which Carol immediately moved to one side causing the warmth to increase. Gillian held out her hands to the blaze whilst Carol went and drew the floor-length curtains and switching on a couple of lamps.

'There!' she said with a satisfied sigh, starting to remove her coat.

Gillian, whilst taking off her own coat, was looking around her. It was a beautiful room, but had a lived-in, comfortable look and feel. The three-piece suite was large with loose covers and deep cushions. There was a desk in the corner, the usual TV and video recorder, music centre, bookshelves and on the fireplace pictures and ornaments. Gillian went to look at the pictures. The first showed two small girls, one about seven, the other maybe a year or two older—arm in arm, both with short, bobbed hair and cheeky grins.

'You and me?' Gillian asked wistfully.

'That's right. And there you are again when

11

you graduated from university.'

She pointed out the photograph of a much older person with shoulder-length hair and a serious expression, wearing a gown and mortar board, the sort of picture that must adorn the mantelpieces of thousands of proud parents.

Thinking this made Gillian say, 'What about our parents, Carol? Where are they?'

Carol's face was serious.

'Well, Dad died when we were little and Mum died before I went to Rumania. I nearly didn't go because I didn't want to leave you alone, but you insisted on it. That's when you moved here.'

'Where did we live before?'

'In Bath. Shall I make some tea?'

She spoke quickly and Gillian had a feeling her sister was trying to change the subject. Perhaps even now talking about their parents upset her. All Gillian could feel at that moment was a deep hurt and frustration that she couldn't remember either of the parents with whom she and Carol had obviously had a close relationship.

'I'd love some tea, thank you,' she said.

Carol smiled.

'Sit down then. Shall I put on some music?'

'No, thanks. I'm quite content to sit and stare at the fire.'

'Lovely, isn't it?' Carol agreed and left her alone.

When she returned later with the tea,

Gillian was still standing in front of the fire. This time she had another picture in her hands. She held it out to Carol.

'Who is this?' she asked, looking at the girl in the picture, with long, curly fair hair and a pale complexion.

Gillian guessed her age to be about seventeen or eighteen. Carol put the tray down on a small table and came and took the photograph from Gillian.

'Oh, that's me,' she said, putting it back on the mantelpiece. 'Come and have one of these delicious chocolate biscuits. They're supposed to be new. I picked them up from the grocer's when I was here this morning.'

Gillian swung round to face the photograph again.

'You?' she repeated. 'But your hair's dark.'

Carol was busy pouring tea into two blue and white cups.

'Yes, I know, and cut short as a boy's. I had a colour change. That's something else you won't be able to remember, Gillian. When you first saw my new look you nearly had a fit.'

Gillian stared hard at her sister.

'Oh, I don't know. The colour and style suit you very well.'

'That's not what you said when I had it cut,' Carol retorted with a grin.

'Well, I've changed my mind.'

Gillian was beginning to relax. So, she couldn't remember much, if anything at all,

13

but she felt comfortable, at peace with herself. She knew she was home. She knew she was safe. She would have to take things one day at a time. This was a good place to be, she felt sure of it. She was also absolutely convinced that she and Carol were as close as two people could possibly be.

'This is my sister,' she said to herself. 'Perhaps my only living relative and I'm sure I love her very much.'

Just then, a strong, emotional feeling overcame her and she caught a surprised Carol in her arms and gave her a warm, fierce hug.

'Oh, Carol, I'm so glad you're here,' she cried.

Carol returned the hug with equal fervour.

'I'll always be here, Gillian,' she promised, 'for as long as you need me.'

It was the next morning at breakfast when Gillian asked, 'By the way, does either of us work for a living?'

It was a question that had come to her out of the blue. They couldn't exactly be poor to be living in a house like this. In such a lovely position, the property wouldn't come cheap in Bourton-on-the-Water.

Carol reached for a slice of toast and began to spread it with butter.

'Yes, you have a job,' she said. 'A career really. You did very well at university and you now have your own business. You're a caterer.'

'A caterer?' Gillian repeated in surprise.

14

'You mean I can cook?'

'You're a marvellous cook. Let you loose in a kitchen and you're in your element.'

'Do you think I'll have forgotten all my skills?' Gillian said anxiously.

If she could continue with her work, even if she couldn't remember a darned thing about it, surely that could be nothing but beneficial for her.

'Of course not. If you could ride a bicycle, and by the way you can't, you wouldn't have forgotten how to, would you? Or how to swim.'

'What exactly do I do?'

She was eagerly curious to find out all she could. Carol picked up the marmalade jar.

'Your firm is simply called Gillian's and you're quite well known. You travel all over the place, working from home, of course.'

'No wonder we have such a fabulous kitchen,' Gillian remarked.

'Exactly. And your speciality is gateaux, gorgeous, mouth-watering, terribly fattening gateaux. You also organise buffets, wedding breakfasts, birthday parties, things like that. Often you do the preparations on your client's premises. Most of them are loaded and you only have to wave your little finger and whatever you need, they supply. Then you charge them a hefty, extortionate sum of money for the privilege of using your services.'

'Am I really as bad as all that?'

Carol stared at her.

15

'There's nothing bad about it. You deserve every penny you get, believe me. You work your fingers to the bone, if necessary.'

'And I do all this by myself?'

It seemed too good to be true.

'Not always. You have outside helpers, as and when necessary. Depends how large the function is. You have a transit van in the garage with your name emblazoned on it, but you only use that if you're actually transporting a large amount of food about.'

'It sounds fascinating.'

Gillian found she felt quite excited by the prospect of taking up her work again.

'And how do you fit in with all this?'

Carol grinned mischieviously.

'Well, I'm a hopeless cook. Hence the mere four-minute, boiled eggs and scorched toast this morning. But I do come along sometimes, to keep you company, to help with the mountains of washing up, or at least, the stacking of dishwashers, but I have my own job, too.'

She paused.

'Yes?'

Gillian waited for another startling revelation.

'Oh, it isn't as exciting as yours, Gillian. I have no skills whatsoever. I work in a charity shop in the village. I don't get paid except for perks and any expenses and I can still claim dole money.'

Gillian tried to hide her disappointment, remembering what her sister had previously told her about doing voluntary overseas work in Rumania, but her expression was not lost on Carol.

'It's only temporary, the job,' she hastened to say. 'And I don't intend to be a burden on the state for the rest of my life, Gillian, but I haven't been home long, you know that.'

'No, I don't,' Gillian reminded her quietly.

'Of course not, I'm sorry, but I haven't. Well, you're going to need time to regain your memory and I'm going to need time to get on my feet again, too. Let's help each other, shall we?'

Her large brown eyes held a sort of desperation and Gillian's love for her rushed to the surface again. She leaned across the table and held Carol's hand.

'I suddenly feel that the future holds nothing but good for both of us, Carol,' she said. 'In fact, I really feel quite excited about it.'

CHAPTER THREE

They didn't do a great deal over the next couple of days. They went for long walks and came back cold and exhausted to the house's welcoming warmth. Gillian also spent some time exploring the village alone. The first time she took the five-minute stroll down to the centre she felt nervous and apprehensive but as soon as she saw the river and the ducks and the little wooden bridges she knew everything was going to be all right.

It wasn't a strange place to her at all! She remembered the village's layout, the shops. She knew where the post office was, and the motor museum that she had always found so fascinating. She knew if she walked along the river bank she would come to Birdland, a vast park which was home to birds of all types, and to penguins that swam about in a glass-sided tank. She knew that in summer, Bourton-on-the-Water was crowded with visitors as indeed were most of the Cotswold villages. Even now in the depth of winter there were people with cameras, taking pictures of anything and everything.

When Carol drove Gillian to the hospital for a follow-up appointment with Dr Morgan, Gillian expressed to him her amazement about being able to remember places but not people or events. He smiled at her.

'That's not uncommon in cases of amnesia such as yours,' he said. 'And it's a very good indication that you will regain your long-term memory one day.'

'One day!' Gillian cried. 'This year, next year, sometime, never, you mean?'

The doctor shrugged his shoulders.

'Patience, Gillian, I urge you to be patient,' he admonished her gently. 'You seem to be in perfect health. Your cuts are healing, your bruises are fading.'

'Yes, I know, Doctor,' Gillian broke in, 'take it one day at a time,' but she was smiling, too, and she left the hospital feeling reasonably optimistic about her future.

She and Carol had decided that they wouldn't tell anybody about her amnesia. It appeared that they were only on nodding acquaintance with their neighbours anyway and whilst in the village, one or two people had bid her a good-day and shopkeepers seemed friendly and polite, there didn't appear to be too many people with whom Gillian and Carol had formed close friendships. Without bothering to be concerned about this, Gillian was grateful that awkward explanations would not be necessary. She found that she was perfectly content with just her sister's company.

On their first evening at home, Carol had said, 'I'm taking a few days leave of absence from the charity shop. And you're not to worry about your work, Gillian. I went through your engagement book and rang people whose parties or whatever were imminent. I told them you'd been in an accident and would be out of commission for a while.'

'That was very thoughtful of you,' Gillian said. 'Thank you, Carol.'

Secretly she wondered if such a move had been a wise one. Surely it would be bad for her business if she had to cancel appointments. Also, wouldn't it be better for her to plunge headlong into her work as soon as possible, to carry on with her normal life? After all, as Dr Morgan had said, she was perfectly healthy. She kept such thoughts to herself, however, not wanting to upset her sister who was being so kind and helpful.

'You mentioned an engagement book,' she did say. 'Where is it? In the desk?'

She glanced at the desk in the corner of the living-room.

'It was,' Carol said, 'but I've moved it for the time being. You mustn't concern yourself with it just yet.'

Gillian knew she could insist on seeing the book, perhaps she ought to, but she didn't. She sighed. She was quickly learning patience. Of course she might well be the sort of person who naturally had the patience of a saint. It would be interesting to find out just what sort of character she did have.

They spent the long, dark evenings either playing Scrabble or watching television and were never very late going to bed. Gillian slept well, no dreams disturbing her, except for one night about a week after she came out of hospital when she awoke to hear sobs and wild cries echoing in her ears.

She sat up abruptly, straining to hear every sound. The room was very dark and she fumbled for the bedside light. There was quite a long silence and she began to wonder if she had indeed been having a bad dream when she heard the cries again. They were coming from Carol's room!

She got up quickly, grabbing her dressing-gown and crossed the dark, chilly hall to her sister's room. She switched on the hall light, fumbling for the switch in the darkness so that she would be able to see Carol without having to put her bedside light on. Carol was tossing about in the bed, her eyes tightly closed, a very worried look on her face. She had kicked the duvet aside and it now lay half on, half off the bed. She was moaning in her sleep.

'No, no,' she kept saying and her face was wet with tears.

Carefully, Gillian pulled the duvet back into position and sat on the edge of the bed before touching Carol lightly on the shoulder. She didn't want to shake her in case it startled her, but she couldn't leave her in such a state. The light touch had an electrifying effect on Carol.

Her eyes shot open and she pushed herself upright in the bed. She saw Gillian sitting there and after a moment of total surprise, she flung her arms around Gillian's neck, hanging on for grim death. She was still sobbing, her sobs muffled against Gillian's shoulder.

'It's all right, it's all right,' Gillian said soothingly, stroking her sister's short hair. 'Just a bad dream. Was it about the accident?'

'No, not that.'

Carol's body shuddered as though she was cold and instinctively Gillian pulled the duvet up around her bare shoulders.

'Then what?'

Gillian probed gently.

'I get nightmares from time to time. Something happened in Rumania. Something bad.'

'Do you want to talk about it?'

Carol shook her head vigorously.

'No, I can't. Please, don't ask me to.'

She pushed her hands through her short hair, causing it to stick up in spikes.

'I'm fine now, really I am.'

She even managed a small grin.

'If you hear me again, just turn over and go back to sleep. It passes.'

'Just tell me one thing,' Gillian urged her. 'Did something bad happen to you, Carol? Is that why you came home?'

'No, not to me. Please, I don't want to talk about it. Go back to bed, please.'

Gillian was reluctant to leave her sister. The sobs and the cries had been so terrible.

'If you're sure you're all right,' she murmured.

'I'm fine.'

It was a long time before Gillian got back to sleep but the next morning Carol was her usual bright, breezy self. She didn't mention the nightmare and consequently Gillian felt unable to mention it either. But she couldn't help thinking that it wasn't only herself who had uncertainties and problems in their life.

Two lame dogs, she thought wryly, helping one another over a stile.

For the next couple of nights, Gillian slept badly because she was half-expecting her sister to have another nightmare, but nothing happened and gradually Gillian found she could drift off to sleep and sleep deeply all night long. Now that she was used to the house and had developed a deep love for her sister, Gillian knew it was time to go one step further and take up the reins of her business life again.

She had experimented in the kitchen and yes, Carol was right, she loved cooking and baking and was extremely good at it. Now she needed to know how capable she was at cooking and baking for other people. She must see her appointment book and take it from there. She approached Carol immediately.

'Please, tell me where my appointment book is,' she said quietly. 'I need it now.'

Carol looked uncertain.

'Are you sure?' she asked.

'Positive. I'm not an invalid, you know. I guess I'm going to have to make several phone calls at the very least. I don't want to lose any of my clients, do I?'

Carol seemed to think for a moment.

'All right,' she said at last, and disappeared into her bedroom, emerging a few moments later with a thick, black-bound book in her hand.

It turned out to be a page-a-day diary. Gillian took it from Carol and held it in her hands simply staring at it.

'You don't have to go back to work just yet, Gillian,' Carol said. 'We're not exactly paupers. Well, at least, you're not,' she ended with a grin.

'Perhaps it's now or never,' Gillian said.

'Well, I'll leave you to it. I think I'll walk down to the charity shop this morning. Show my face. Is that OK?'

'Of course. Will you be back for lunch?'

'Probably. I only work part-time and they're pretty flexible.'

Gillian waited till Carol had put on her coat and a jaunty red beret and knee-length brown boots, then waved to her sister as she walked down the road. The breakfast dishes were stacked in the dishwasher, the beds were made and she had already vacuumed. Nothing much else to do for the time being. Gillian took the diary into the sitting-room, and made herself comfortable on the couch. Then, almost holding her breath, she opened the diary.

She was amazed at the amount of writing that was crammed into the pages, seemingly for many months ahead. This was worse than she had thought! Then she realised the advance bookings were not something to fear but were merely indications that her business, as Carol had told her, was doing really well. Surely she need only be pleased about this.

The first signs showed that most of the bookings were in the Gloucestershire or Wiltshire areas so they would not involve a great deal of travelling. There were names, addresses and telephone numbers and hastily-scribbled notes she herself must have made, sample menus and in some cases merely menu ideas.

It was interesting to see what her handwriting looked like and for the first time in days Gillian felt a sense of panic spreading over her. What if it was always like this? What if she never remembered?

Quickly she pulled herself together. She wouldn't think like that. Of course she would remember. Dr Morgan had promised her she would. Well, not exactly promised but he'd certainly been cheerfully optimistic and so must she. She turned back the pages of the diary to the present time. Whatever bookings had been listed for the days since her accident could not be helped.

She knew Carol had made telephone calls and, of course, she would follow these up with calls or letters, or perhaps even visits of her own. It was all a matter of grabbing her courage in both hands and going for it!

She remembered she had left hospital on February twenty-second, which was a Thursday and that she had been in there for three days and nights, so the accident must have occurred on Monday, February nineteenth. As she and Carol had been returning from the theatre in Cheltenham at the time it was quite possible that she had not had an appointment on that day, but she had to make sure. Perhaps that was one event that had gone ahead as planned. It could well have taken place earlier in the day, leaving her a free evening to go to Cheltenham with her sister.

Her brow creased as she checked the pages and went from Sunday, eighteenth February to Tuesday, February twentieth which was, of course her first day in hospital. What had happened to Monday, nineteenth? Closer inspection revealed that a page had been torn out of the diary, leaving only a few tattered shreds close to the binding. Now why should she tear a page from her engagement book? It didn't make sense.

She closed the book but held it in her hands. When she heard the front door opening and closing and realised that Carol was already back, she jumped up and went to greet her.

Carol smiled.

'I forgot, silly me. The charity shop closes on Tuesdays.'

She gave a shudder as she removed her thick, woolly gloves.

'Gosh, it's freezing out there. Had your morning coffee yet, Gillian?'

'No, not yet.'

She looked at her watch. It was only just after ten. A bit early for coffee but she followed Carol into the kitchen and watched her putting on the kettle even before she removed her coat and boots. Carol turned round and leaned against the worktop.

'Is something wrong? You look worried. Now I told you it was too early for you to busy your head with appointments and such!'

Gillian still held the diary in her hands. She opened it at the missing page.

'Do you know anything about this?' she asked.

'About what?'

Carol bent down and removed her boots.

'There's been a page torn out of my diary, the day of the accident.'

'So what? Are you asking me if I tore the page out?'

Was she doing that? How preposterous if she was. Why would Carol want to mutilate the diary any more than she herself would?

27

'Well, someone certainly has and I know it wasn't me,' she found herself saying.

Carol slipped her winter coat off her shoulders and moved past Gillian to hang it in the hallrobe.

'Oh, you know it wasn't you, do you?' she said and Gillian was sure she didn't imagine the sharp note in her sister's voice. 'So, your memory's returned, has it?'

'No,' she said quietly, putting the diary on the worktop.

'Oh, Gillian, I'm sorry, that was cruel of me.'

Carol came immediately and put her arm round Gillian's shoulders.

'I didn't mean to speak so sharply. But, honestly, I haven't the faintest idea why there's a page missing from your book. Perhaps it was a spoiled page, and if there wasn't anything important on it, perhaps you tore it out yourself and threw it away. Couldn't that be it?'

Gillian knew that it could and that that was the most likely explanation. She didn't know why she was making such a fuss about it. Even if the missing day had been the most important day of her life, she couldn't remember it and it was too late to do anything about it now. She tried to smile.

'Let's forget about it, shall we?' she suggested. 'And, yes, I'd love some coffee, please, and a couple of those chocolate biscuits if there are any left.'

Carol seemed to relax.

'I bought three packets,' she confessed.

But Gillian was unable to forget about the page. It niggled her. She knew she was blowing the matter up out of all proportion but she couldn't help it. With her mind and her memory being mostly like an empty void with nothing to fill it up, the incident of the missing diary page seemed to loom large and foreboding in Gillian's existence.

She began to search for what must be a very small, crumpled piece of paper. She could imagine it, lying in a forgotten corner somewhere, or in the back of a drawer though why if she had torn out the page she should then go on to save it she had no idea. It became almost an obsession with her and because she knew Carol would be dismissive about what she was doing, or maybe even cross, she didn't say anything to her sister.

As it happened, Carol seemed to be spending more and more time away from the house. She went to the charity shop sometimes but she also spent time at one of the local pubs where she said she had met a group of new friends.

'You don't mind if I go out sometimes, do you, Gillian?' she had asked the first time.

'Of course not,' Gillian assured her.

She knew that her sister was only twenty-three, two years younger than she was.

Birthdays were something they had discussed very early on. Gillian was also beginning to realise that her sister had a very gregarious and restless nature. The quiet evenings they had spent together had soon begun to pall with Carol, so Gillian was glad she had found some friends. As for herself, well, she wasn't yet ready to take up any sort of social life, even if she should have had the most crowded of social calendars before her accident, which she very much doubted.

She used her time alone to make several apologetic phone calls, explaining about the accident, though not the loss of memory and was pleased and touched that most people she contacted were very understanding and more concerned about her welfare than their own disrupted plans. She also baked cakes and gateaux for the freezer which was an enormous one and prepared many other dishes in readiness for her return to business.

The rest of the time was spent searching for that elusive piece of paper. It was about then that Gillian discovered two facts. One was that the top, left-hand drawer of the desk in the living-room was locked and she could not find a key to open it no matter how many keys from the bunch hanging in the kitchen that she tried, and the other was that the photograph of Carol as a teenager had disappeared from the mantelpiece.

When Carol returned home much later one

night, Gillian tackled her about both matters.

'I don't suppose you know where the key to the top drawer in the desk is kept?' she asked as casually as she could.

'I haven't the faintest idea,' Carol returned.

Gillian could see that her sister was a little high. Her enormous dark eyes were bright and glittering and she had a tendency to giggle.

'It must be locked for a reason,' Gillian remarked.

'Obviously, but it's your desk, Gillian, not mine. I've got my own bureau in my bedroom, haven't I?'

Carol flung herself down on the couch and lay full length with her eyes closed.

'It's a beautiful night,' she sighed. 'A sky full of stars!'

'I don't suppose it's any use asking you about the missing photograph either, is it?' Gillian went on.

Carol didn't open her eyes.

'What photograph?'

'The one of you on the mantelpiece that I looked at the day I came out of hospital.'

Languidly, Carol brought herself to a sitting position.

'Oh, that!' she drawled. 'Guilty! I knocked it off and the glass broke. I've got it in my bag somewhere and I'm going to get a new piece of glass for it. OK?'

She promptly lay down again, closed her eyes and within seconds was deep in sleep.

31

Gillian stared down fondly at her sister. She looked so young, younger than her years. Gillian felt somehow responsible for her. She knew Carol had said many times that she would look after Gillian, but Gillian felt the truth was the other way around. It was hard to believe Carol had spent at least a couple of years doing charity work abroad.

Anyway, Gillian thought, I have a reasonable explanation for the disappearance of the photograph but the locked drawer continued to remain a mystery and there continued to be no sign of the diary's missing page.

CHAPTER FOUR

'Gillian,' Carol began one morning about a week later, 'would you mind awfully if I went away for a few days?'

'Away? Where to?'

'Stratford. A few of my friends are going and asked me if I'd like to join them. I said I'd have to check with you first.'

Gillian smiled.

'You can do what you like and go where you like, Carol, you know that,' she said. 'You don't have to ask my permission.'

Carol bent to fasten the laces on her boots. Most of the snow had gone by now but it was still very slushy underfoot.

'Yes, I do. Well, at least, I have to consider you. I promised I'd take care of you, didn't I?'

'I don't need any taking care of,' Gillian assured her. 'I'm fine now. I've done two parties and have another one tonight. I'm coping very well.'

True, she still hadn't remembered a single detail about her past, but she was feeling very well in herself. Her confidence had returned.

'I know that, and I'm so happy for you,' Carol said. 'If you're quite sure?'

'I'm positive. Go on and enjoy yourself. Will you go to the theatre?'

'I expect so.'

Carol straightened up and pushed her hands into the pockets of her trousers.

'There's just one other thing.' She sounded very hesitant.

'Yes?' Gillian queried.

'I haven't any money. Well, not enough. I hate to ask you for money, Gillian.'

Gillian laughed.

'Don't be silly. I know your dole money won't go far.'

Carol looked at her.

'I'm not drawing dole,' she said.

'But you said you were!'

'I know. I lied. I couldn't let you know I didn't have any money, not when you were, well, not quite yourself. That would have been awful of me. But I couldn't bring myself to sign on, and at first it didn't matter because I didn't really need any money, but now . . .'

She seemed so embarrassed and Gillian hated to see her sister that way. It would give her great pleasure to give money to Carol.

'I'll give you some money on one condition,' she said.

Carol looked doubtful.

'And what's that?'

'It isn't to be a loan. I'll make you a monthly allowance until you can find yourself a proper job. It's the least I can do.'

Carol was overjoyed.

'Oh, thank you, Gillian, thank you,' she enthused. 'I won't forget this, I promise.'

From then on she was like an excited child as she talked non-stop about the proposed holiday in Stratford. Once she had left, Gillian did have one small regret—that Carol had not seen fit to introduce any of her friends. A car had pulled up at the gate, a horn was sounded and Carol was off with a swift hug and a cheery wave. The house seemed quiet and empty without her and Gillian scolded herself for feeling anxious.

Carol would be fine. Then she threw herself with renewed vigour into preparing more cakes and planning more menus.

On the second day of Carol's absence, Gillian went into her sister's bedroom to put away a pile of newly-ironed clothes. She stood in the doorway looking around in horror. The bedroom was a tip! The bed was unmade, drawers were half open, as was the wardrobe and the dressing-table was crowded with everything from handcream jars to make-up to discarded underwear.

Well, her first job of the morning would be to give the bedroom a thorough clean. She herself was a very tidy person; obviously her sister was not! So that was something else she had learned. She made the bed and picked up the strewn items of clothing, depositing them in the linen basket in the bathroom. She fetched the vacuum cleaner and a duster and put them to good use.

Finally, she started to put away the pile of

fresh laundry, generally tidying drawers and shelves as she did so. There seemed to be an odd diversity of clothing, old T-shirts and jeans alongside quite expensive-looking sweaters and skirts. It was almost as though two different people were occupying the room, one who took care of her clothes and one who did not.

In the bottom of the wardrobe was another jumble of unwashed clothing. As Gillian gathered it together, feeling a little cross with Carol for the way she had treated some delicate, expensive-looking items, she saw the crumpled piece of white paper on the bottom of the wardrobe.

Immediately the sheet torn from her diary sprang to mind. She picked it up and opened it out. It was the missing page! There was the date Monday, February 19. She read what was written there. *Owen. Bridge Cottage, Hallfield Farm, nr Helmsley, North Yorks. ASAP.*

Abruptly Gillian sat down on the edge of the bed staring at the piece of crumpled paper. It must be the details of a booking, what else could it be? But what was it doing in the bottom of Carol's wardrobe? Why had she torn the sheet out in the first place and then hidden it? But, of course, it wasn't really hidden, just tossed carelessly in there along with everything else and then probably forgotten about. One thing seemed certain— Carol hadn't wanted Gillian to know about that day's booking. She had deliberately lied about it.

On the day of the accident Gillian mustn't have gone to Yorkshire. She had been to Cheltenham with Carol. So had the booking been cancelled? And why would she have taken a booking so far away from home? There were no other bookings in her diary in that area of the country.

She quickly finished off the bedroom and went into the kitchen to make some tea, sitting at the table, her mind churning with all sorts of unanswered questions, the smoothed-out piece of paper in front of her. Owen. Oh, how frustrating it was not being able to remember! There was no phone number so she couldn't ring up. Anyway, she didn't know if she wanted to phone. What could she say?

But she had to know the truth. She had to find out and she knew there was only one way to do it. She had to go to Yorkshire, find this Bridge Cottage. The visit could prove very beneficial to her. It might help her to regain her memory. There had been no more snow, so the motorways and main roads would be clear.

Gillian got up, leaving her tea half drunk and went into the living-room to get the road atlas which she knew was on the top of her desk. She didn't have to worry about Carol for the time being. In fact, it might be better if she put her sister completely out of her mind as she was beginning to have serious concerns about her. No, she would set off for Yorkshire that very day. Luckily she had no immediate engagements and had everything prepared for the next one due.

Packing took Gillian no time at all and she had her own car now, a new one to replace the one that was written off. She reckoned she could reach North Yorkshire in about three to three and a half hours. She wouldn't give too much consideration to what awaited her at her journey's end, but would sit back and enjoy the trip.

Finding the small market town of Helmsley was no trouble and the journey had proved uneventful. She had stopped only once at a motorway service station. Travelling farther north had not, as Gillian had feared, taken her into worsening weather and here, too, only a smattering of snow remained. It had been a clear day and because of her fairly early start it wasn't yet dark when she reached Helmsley.

However, by the time she came across first Hallfield Farm itself and then Bridge Cottage which seemed to be situated within the farm's boundaries, it had become quite dark and because of the sudden appearance of low cloud and no moon, only the car's headlights helped to illuminate Gillian's path. She had asked directions twice and had been on the point of despair when she saw the farm's sign.

It was in complete darkness which didn't

increase Gillian's confidence. Perhaps she should have booked for a night's bed and breakfast in Helmsley and come out here in the morning, but it was too late to go back.

The cottage seemed to loom suddenly out of the darkness just after she had crossed over a stream by way of a hump-backed bridge which must have given the cottage its name. Thankfully a welcoming light beamed from one of the downstairs windows and there was also an exterior light over the door. Outside, a Range Rover was parked and as Gillian approached, she heard a dog begin to bark. Well, here goes, she thought, wishing for the first time that she had never come and feeling it was all going to be a complete waste of time. Resolutely she banged loudly on the door.

After a few moments the dog's barking grew louder as though an inner door had been opened and Gillian could hear a man's voice as he fumbled with a key or a bolt inside the door. Then the door was opened. Light from the hall spilled out and illuminated Gillian. A small brown-and-white mongrel dog rushed out to greet her, no longer barking but wagging its tail and seeming generally glad to see her.

'Rob, stop that!'

The voice was firm but not angry. He peered out at Gillian and she saw a tall, slenderly-built man in his late twenties or early thirties, perhaps, with dark hair, wearing a dark green sweater over dark trousers.

She wasn't prepared for the way his face suddenly flooded with recognition as he flung the door wider open.

'Gillian! Good gracious where did you spring from?'

Nor was she prepared for the way he caught her in his arms and kissed her full on the mouth!

CHAPTER FIVE

Gillian struggled to free herself and when she managed to do so she stood back from the young man and faced him angrily.

'Mr Owen!' she cried. 'How dare you treat me like that!'

In the background she could hear the dog barking excitedly. The man regarded her with complete amazement.

'Mr Owen?' he repeated. 'What on earth's the matter with you, Gillian? Look, you'd better come in.'

He stood to one side, but she was about to turn and walk back to her car when, in that instant, it dawned on her. He knew her! And he obviously knew her extremely well, and what is more she must know him in more than simply a passing fashion. She had come here in the first place to try to aid the return of her memory. She couldn't run away.

She turned back to see him staring at her, waiting, with a look of complete bewilderment on his face. It was a nice face, a friendly, kind face, good-looking, too, with brown eyes and a lot of soft brown hair worn rather long. She knew instinctively she had nothing to fear from this man and perhaps had much to gain.

'Yes, I will come in, thank you,' she said quietly.

The greeting of the dog did not bother her. She had never owned a dog but liked them nevertheless. She made a fuss of him until the man made a brief command and the dog retreated to lie in front of the roaring fire, watching the pair of them with eager eyes.

'Take your coat off, Gillian, and sit down,' he said. 'Would you like something to drink? Coffee? Tea? Hot chocolate?'

'Nothing, thanks, for the moment,' Gillian said, shaking her head.

Actually hot chocolate sounded wonderful but she was bursting inside with tension and nervousness. She wouldn't have been able to do the chocolate justice.

He came and sat in a chair opposite her. He had long legs which he stretched out in front of him. His glance was no more than polite and curious. No-one would have guessed that only minutes before he had been kissing her so intimately. At the memory, Gillian felt her cheeks reddening and told herself it was because of the heat of the fire. She glanced about her. It was a cosy, comfortable room, low-ceilinged. She imagined this man must have to be very careful not to keep banging his head when he came in and out of doors!

'Don't you think you owe me an explanation, Gillian?' he said presently.

She looked at him, then immediately looked away again, staring at her hands.

'First,' she began, carefully choosing her

words, 'please, will you answer me one question?'

'If I can.'

'It may sound a ridiculous question, but nonetheless I must ask it.'

'Fire away.'

He actually smiled. He was quite handsome and inspired confidence in Gillian.

He sat up straight from his lounging position and drew in his long legs.

'Oh, come on, Gillian!' he said in an exasperated voice.

'No, please. You see, I don't know you at all. At least I can't remember having known you. I was in a car accident recently and I've lost my memory. That's why I'm here. I found your name and address in my diary.'

There! It was said now. No other explanation was necessary. The ball was in his court. When he got up and came to sit by her on the low couch she flinched slightly in case he should try to take her in his arms again but all he did was to take hold of her hand. She didn't pull away from him. The pressure of his warm fingers was comforting.

'Darling, how ghastly for you,' he said. 'So that's why you addressed me as Mr Owen. Owen's my first name, Gillian.'

It didn't ring any bells, but then she had known it wouldn't.

'Owen Palmer. I'm so sorry about your accident. When did it happen? Can you

43

remember that?' he continued.

'Oh, yes, I can remember everything that happened after I came round in hospital, but not a thing about myself that went before. I'm having to learn as I go, piece by painstaking piece. For instance, I know I'm a caterer by profession and when I saw your name and address in my engagement diary I thought I must have been here on February nineteenth to do some sort of party for a family called Owen, though for the life of me I couldn't think why I'd come all the way up here from Gloucestershire to do that.'

She looked at him. He was regarding her solemnly.

'That's where I live, Bourton-on-the-Water, in Gloucestershire.'

He gave her another of his dazzling smiles.

'I know where you live, Gillian,' he said. 'I lived there myself for a while. I had an antique shop. That's how we met, you and I, and that's where we fell in love.'

He watched her carefully for her reaction to his words. She said nothing and he went on, giving her fingers a squeeze.

'Why else would I have embraced you like I did? I'm not in the habit of kissing perfect strangers who turn up on my doorstep in the middle of the night.'

In spite of herself and the way she was feeling at that moment Gillian found she was smiling, too.

44

'It's hardly the middle of the night,' she argued.

'No, it just seems like that with the curtains drawn and the sky as black as a witch's hat. When was your accident, by the way?'

'On that Monday night, the nineteenth.'

His eyebrows rose slightly.

'On the same day you left here then? When it started to snow, I felt certain you'd have got home by then. At least, I hoped you would have.'

'Yes, I must have, because I went to the theatre in Cheltenham, apparently, and it was whilst I was driving back from there that the car skidded and I hit a tree.'

Owen frowned.

'Are you sure you went to the theatre on the Monday? I would have thought that to be highly improbable, if not impossible, considering the time you left here.'

'Yes, I'm sure.'

But was she? Perhaps she had misunderstood Carol. Perhaps she had missed a day somewhere. She wasn't really too sure about anything.

'Well,' Owen began, 'thank goodness you weren't badly hurt.'

'Unless you call not knowing a thing about yourself being badly hurt,' Gillian responded.

'I tried to phone you, you know, on the Tuesday after you left and again on the Wednesday, and I left messages on your answering machine.'

'I never got the messages. The machine must be faulty.'

But she had used it since she came out of hospital and it was fine.

Owen smiled.

'I must confess I wondered why you hadn't been in touch, but I wasn't really worried. I knew how busy you always were.'

Gillian tried to shake off worrying images surrounding her accident.

'You said you used to live in Bourton. Why, if we'd fallen in love, had you moved up here?'

For a moment Owen's face seemed to cloud over. He got up and made a pretence of poking the fire which was blazing away quite merrily. Rob, the dog, made a tentative move but soon settled back on the hearth rug when Owen sat down again.

'My family lives in Helmsley. There was a family crisis and I had to come back. But I asked you to come up here because I wanted to ask you to marry me.'

Here was another shock.

Gillian managed to ask, 'And did you?'

'Oh, yes, and you said you would. I gave you a ring.'

Slowly he lifted her left hand.

'Why aren't you wearing it now, Gillian? Have you lost it? The ring on your engagement finger might have helped to trigger off your memory perhaps.'

Gillian stared at her naked fingers.

'I don't know what happened to it. I'm sorry. Perhaps I lost it when the car crashed. Oh, Owen,' she said, using his name for the first time, 'isn't this all a terrible mess?'

She allowed him to put his arm around her shoulders. She even rested her head against him. He didn't feel like a stranger to her. There was something about him that she trusted implicitly.

'I should have insisted you stay here on that Monday,' he said, 'but, no, you had pressing engagements. You were always so busy, Gillian, and loyal to your clients. We had both resigned ourselves to being apart for a while, meeting when we could. It wasn't enough, but you had your work and I . . .'

He broke off.

'Well, we won't go into that now. Later, perhaps. Just now I'm going to make you something to eat and put a bottle in the spare bed. You certainly can't travel back tonight.'

'But I can't stay here,' Gillian protested.

'Of course you can and it isn't open for debate.'

Owen's voice was firm.

'Would I be so utterly stupid as to let you disappear into the night? Oh, no. You're here and I don't care whether you have a dozen parties booked for tomorrow, here is where you're going to stay, at least, for a while.'

She was surprised when he leaned forward

and kissed her cheek lightly.

'We need to get to know one another all over again.'

He stood head and shoulders over her so she had to raise her face to look at him. The thought of laying down her head on what she knew would be a supremely comfortable pillow in this little cottage with Owen playing the part of guardian angel was very tempting. She had nothing to go back for. Carol was away and there were no pressing engagements as Owen had put it, not for the next couple of days anyway. She had even brought a small overnight bag with her just on the off chance.

As if reading her mind, Owen said, 'Did you bring a bag with you, by any chance?'

Gillian nodded.

'In my car.'

Owen held out his hand.

'Then give me the key and I'll get it for you.'

She took the car keys from her coat pocket and, whistling for the dog to follow him, Owen went outside. Gillian sat, leaning her head against a cushion and staring at the fire. One day at a time, she reminded herself, wondering if indeed she would be able to sleep with so much going on in her head.

Owen returned in less than a minute. Gillian opened her eyes and saw he was covered in soft white flakes.

'It's snowing like mad,' he told her, 'so I couldn't have let you leave, could I?'

He grinned.

*   *   *

The narrow bed was warm and comfortable, a hot-water bottle toasting her toes. The night around her was silent. She had looked out of the bedroom window at the gently-falling snow which had already covered the ground and was settling on the trees. The clouds had cleared and there was a bright moon. The nearby stream glided by like a twisting black ribbon between its snow-covered banks. Perhaps they would become snowbound! Perhaps, Gillian thought, such a prospect should have alarmed her, but it didn't. Instead she found it exciting and challenging. As Owen had said, they needed to get to know one another all over again.

She had loved this man enough to want to marry him. Now he was a stranger to her. It was a weird situation, one that seemed hard to handle. She curled up in the bed and heard Owen climbing the narrow stairway. His footsteps creaked as he walked along the landing, past the door of her room. Gillian found that she was holding her breath. The footsteps passed by and presently silence returned.

Eventually Gillian fell into a deep sleep, safe and secure in the knowledge that Owen Palmer would be kind, considerate, patient and understanding. Tomorrow she would be able to spend more time with him. It was a lovely thought.

Next day, the air was crystal clear and bitingly cold but they went for a long walk, tramping through the snow which had stopped some time during the night but not before it had become quite thick. Rob was in his element bounding ahead and snuffling in the snow drifts. It was the happiest and most relaxed Gillian had been since her accident. Not one vestige of her memory had returned but here, in this winter wonderland, it didn't seem to matter.

She walked along hand in hand with Owen and knew one thing; that she liked him very much. How could she do otherwise? He was amusing, tender and attentive. He was also a brilliant cook and though admitting that because of her profession he ought to bow to her superior skills, he refused to do anything of the sort.

Over the time she was there, he produced appetising, mouth-watering meals, simple meals which they ate from a low table in front of the fire. When he felt like a break Owen took Gillian into Helmsley for lunch or dinner in one of the pubs around the market square. He showed her his antique shop where he produced a sign on a piece of string that he hung in the window—**Closed for a few days**.

Their conversation was always easy. Owen

made no demands on her and she began to see how easily she must have fallen in love with him. Occasionally her conscience pricked her when she thought of all she could be doing back home, but she could not seem to drag herself away from Owen and he never mentioned there would come a time when she would have to return to Bourton-on-the-Water.

But Carol would be home soon. Gillian knew her days at the cottage, if for that reason alone, were numbered. It would be a wrench, she knew that but surely not the end of her relationship with Owen. She couldn't let him go out of her life now. When it came to her quite starkly that life would be bleak without him, Gillian knew she was falling in love with him all over again. But perhaps it was more than that. Her mind had forgotten him but deep in the core of her being she felt she herself had never forgotten him.

It was a lovely feeling. She spoke nothing of her secret thoughts and hopes, content to be Owen's friend. Sometimes he kissed her, but only in the gentlest and most brotherly of ways and this was enough for her. Indeed she loved Owen all the more because of his gentleness and consideration.

On the fourth day, whilst they were out walking, it started to rain, a heavy downpour that took them completely by surprise. They hurried back to the cottage, their footsteps squelching through the thawing snow. When they got home they were soaking and Gillian was shivering. The bright, refreshing crispness had been one thing but now the cold seemed to seep into her very bones.

'Have a hot bath and I'll make us a drink,' Owen advised.

'Good idea,' Gillian agreed and, discarding her wet outer things, she ran up the stairs to the tiny bathroom.

There always seemed to be lashings of piping hot water and she had a long, lazy soak, feeling the warmth returning to her limbs before reluctantly dragging herself out of the bath and getting dried and dressed in fresh clothing. She never went anywhere without her hairdryer and she sat on the bed drying her long hair and brushing it vigorously before she left the bedroom in anticipation of a mug of delicious hot chocolate.

As she stepped out on to the narrow landing she heard voices, Owen's and someone else's. She hesitated. Had Owen got a visitor? Going back into her bedroom, Gillian glanced out of the window which overlooked the front of the cottage. There was a dark blue car parked out there. The noise of her hairdryer must have masked its arrival. She didn't know whether to go downstairs or wait till the visitor had gone. Back on the landing, she hesitated a little longer, trying to decide what to do. Then she heard a woman's voice speaking very loudly.

'We're never going to find her, Owen. These leads we keep getting are useless.'

Next came a man's voice, not Owen's.

'Diana, don't get upset. Of course we'll find her.'

'No, we won't! We should never have opposed her. If we'd let her have her own way, this would never have happened.'

The man sounded angry, too, now.

'But the fellow dumped her, don't forget that. That's what started it all, not because we tried to make her see sense. Fat lot of good that did.'

Owen spoke next, whilst Gillian stood there, thinking she ought to go back into her bedroom. Whatever was going on downstairs had nothing to do with her.

'Mother, Dad's right,' Owen was saying. 'There's no sense in getting upset. But I do believe this private detective lark is a complete waste of time.. It's my belief Stephanie will come back when she's had enough of trying to fend for herself.'

'And in the meantime,' the older woman yelled back, 'anything might happen to her. She's wild and headstrong and the doctors said . . . oh, I'm at my wits' end.'

Without warning, the door at the bottom of the stairs opened and Gillian saw the woman start to run up the stairs. She ducked into her bedroom doorway but not before she saw that Owen's mother, for this was plainly who it was,

was a tall, blonde-haired woman wearing an expensive fur jacket over a calf-length dark dress or skirt. She glanced upwards and Gillian knew she had been spotted. Then they were facing one another. Mrs Palmer had tears in her eyes and wet on her cheeks. She was a very attractive woman and had Owen's dark eyes.

'Who on earth are you?' she demanded in a rude voice for which Gillian was prepared to make allowances under the circumstances.

'I'm Gillian Avery,' Gillian began. 'I'm a friend of Owen's.'

Mrs Palmer frowned.

'Gillian? Owen's fiancée?'

Before Gillian could speak again, Owen had bounded up the stairs.

'Mother, Gillian arrived unexpectedly the other night,' he explained. 'Come downstairs and I'll tell you all about it. Let me make you some tea.'

Mrs Palmer gave Gillian a weak smile.

'I'm sorry I sounded so rude, but I'm rather upset.'

'That's all right,' Gillian said.

'Come on, Mother,' Owen coaxed, leading her gently downstairs, looking over his shoulder to give Gillian a fond glance.

Slowly she followed them downstairs. She felt nervous. This was a development she could not have envisaged. Clearly Owen intended telling his parents about her amnesia and she wasn't sure she wanted him to. She

54

was still trying to adjust to her new state and although being with Owen had helped she would have preferred that they be alone for the rest of her stay here.

Now she would have to be polite to Mr and Mrs Palmer. And what was all that about someone called Stephanie who had caused Mrs Palmer, at least, great distress? She remembered Owen telling her he had had to leave Bourton-on-the-Water because of a family crisis. He hadn't said just how long ago this had been but surely it was possible that Stephanie, whoever she was, figured in this crisis somewhere.

Once downstairs, Owen introduced Gillian formally to his parents. They shook hands.

Dan Palmer, a tall, well-built man with a friendly smile and curly grey hair said, 'We've heard about you of course, Gillian. Sorry we didn't get to meet you when you came up a few weeks ago. How are you?'

'I'm fine,' Gillian said.

Owen came and put his arm around her.

'Gillian's been through quite an ordeal! Do you mind if I tell them about it, Gillian?'

She did mind but could hardly say so.

'No, of course not.'

She sat down on the couch and Mrs Palmer, after dabbing at her eyes surreptitiously with a lacy handkerchief, came to sit beside her.

'Have you been ill, Gillian?' she asked.

'Not exactly ill, Mother,' Owen began and

went on to tell all he knew about Gillian's accident and amnesia and how she had come to arrive at the cottage like she had.

The Palmers were full of sympathy and for a while at least, Gillian could see that Diana Palmer had put aside her own worries to be concerned about Gillian's own welfare. By the time Owen's parents left for home later that day, not another word had been said about the mysterious Stephanie. Mrs Palmer was cheerful and friendly and it was as if Gillian had never heard her wild words and seen her tears.

CHAPTER SIX

Almost as soon as Owen had closed the door on the departing car, he came to Gillian and said, 'Did you hear anything of what my parents were saying earlier by any chance?'

'Some,' Gillian admitted. 'I couldn't help it. I was coming downstairs and then your mother appeared as she did.'

Owen smiled.

'Don't worry, love, I wasn't reproaching you,' he told her. 'But I expect you're wondering who Stephanie is.'

'Well, yes, wouldn't you be?'

Owen added another log to the fire. Gillian waited patiently on the settee. She was pondering about their forthcoming visit to the Palmers' home. Owen's parents had invited them for an evening meal the following day.

'Just to welcome you to the family, Gillian,' Diana Palmer had said, but Gillian did not know whether she was yet ready to be a member of the family.

Surely Mr and Mrs Palmer, and Owen, too, must realise she wasn't in a position to move too much into the future, not until she had sorted out her past. She brushed such thoughts away for the time being and concentrated on what Owen was saying.

'Stephanie is my sister, Gillian. She's

nineteen and my parents have spoiled her rotten. She's very bright but she's never had a job, never been to university or college, except for a secretarial college where she spent a couple of years. She was supposed to get a job as a secretary, at least that was the general idea, but that sort of job was much too boring for Stephanie. I think she worked for about a week in a solicitors' office then chucked it in. No matter, she didn't have to work. My parents are fairly well off and Stephanie only had to ask to get.'

Owen broke off and gave Gillian a rueful grin.

'Am I sounding cruel?' he asked.

'No, not really.'

'I don't mean to do. I love Stephanie dearly and I expect I was as much to blame as anybody for spoiling her. I was ten when she was born and I doted on her. She was such a beautiful baby.'

His voice had taken on a wistful note. Then in the next breath he resumed his story.

'Well, about six months ago she got involved with a much older, married man. It was the usual story, his wife didn't understand him, he was going to leave her and marry Stephanie and she fell for it, hook, line and sinker. She didn't attempt to keep it a secret from us. In fact, she bragged about it. But, of course, it all fell through. The wife found out about the relationship, the husband begged her forgiveness and dropped Stephanie like a hot brick.

'She had been so sure of him that she'd even bought a wedding dress and she took it pretty badly when he told her it was over. She had a nervous breakdown, and was constantly having nightmares where she would wake up sobbing her heart out. My parents were desperate to keep everything private, within the family. My mother does a lot of charity work, she's on umpteen committees and though they had a doctor coming privately to the house, they wouldn't let Stephanie go to hospital. They wouldn't listen to what I had to say and so what happened was inevitable, I daresay.'

'What did happen, Owen?' Gillian asked quietly, fearing the worst.

'Stephanie ran away. She was supposed to be on medication that made her sleep a great deal, but whether she wasn't taking it as she should, I couldn't say. All I know is one minute she was in bed, the next she had gone. My mother was at her wits' end. We searched everywhere but there was no trace of her.'

'Did you inform the police?'

'No, we didn't. At first I wanted to but my mother refused. She was afraid it might get into the papers. But when my father pointed out that because Stephanie was nineteen, the police would more than likely do nothing at all, I realised he was right. Lots of young people leave home without saying where they are going, I'm sure. We couldn't legally force Stephanie to come home against her will.'

'But if she was ill . . .' Gillian began.

'Yes, I know. Perhaps we were wrong. Anyway, my parents hired a private detective. That's what they were talking about just now. They'd been following up another supposed sighting, another dead end, I'm afraid.'

'You came back here from Bourton because of Stephanie, didn't you?' Gillian asked him.

'That's right. My mother begged me to come home, so I sold my shop and did as she wanted. I wanted to tell you but she wouldn't let me. I was so afraid I might lose you, Gillian.'

He took hold of her hand. Gillian said nothing. In effect, he had lost her and she had lost him when she lost her memory, but it wasn't too late for them. She had to believe that. In that moment whilst Owen was confiding in her as he was she realised how very important it was for her to be able to 'find' Owen again.

'When did Stephanie run away?' she asked him gently. 'Was it long ago?'

'No, only a couple of weeks actually, the day we had that last heavy snow storm.'

He broke off and stared at her.

'The day you came here, Gillian. Of course it was. I remember now. You hadn't been long gone when my mother phoned to say that Stephanie was missing. Now isn't that a

60

coincidence?'

It certainly was, Gillian thought and wished with all her heart that she could remember what had happened the day she left Owen.

* * *

The Palmers lived in a large, detached house set in its own grounds on the other side of Helmsley from Owen's cottage. Gillian had no idea what Dan Palmer did for a living but if the house was anything to go by he must be earning a great deal of money.

Gillian felt very nervous as Owen parked the Range Rover and came to open the door for her. He laughed at her expression.

'No-one's going to bite you, Gillian,' he teased.

'If I'd known I would be invited out to such a house I would have brought something more appropriate to wear,' she said.

'Nonsense! You look wonderful. If I gave you the impression my parents were snobbish and stand-offish I'm sorry. They're not like that at all. I know they've been longing to have you visit. If it hadn't been for Stephanie you'd probably have come here when we got engaged.'

Gillian didn't want to think about either Stephanie or her engagement to Owen. She had moments of great guilt when she remembered she had lost the ring Owen had given her. She had no idea even what sort of a ring it was.

'We won't have to talk about Stephanie all the time will we, Owen?' she asked.

'I hope not. My parents will probably be glad of the opportunity not to talk about her for a while.'

He took her arm and steered her towards the front door. The house was warm and welcoming, as were Diana and Dan Palmer themselves. Diana kissed her cheek and Dan helped her off with her coat. Then they went into the drawing-room. The whole of Owen's cottage would probably have fitted into this one room alone. There were no dogs, which surprised Gillian somewhat, but there were two cats, Siamese, who sat majestic and aloof side by side in one of the deep-cushioned armchairs.

'Meet Suki and Saki,' Diana said.

'Will they let me stroke them?' Gillian asked.

'They'll be your friends for life if you do,' Diana assured her.

So, though both the cats and Owen's mother had appeared rather awesome at first sight, they were nothing of the kind and when Gillian sat down, one of the cats, Suki, she thought, leaped immediately on to her lap purring loudly and contentedly. The other one made itself comfortable on Owen's lap.

Making a fuss of the cats who were

obviously deeply loved by both Mr and Mrs Palmer and Owen, too, helped to break the ice and Gillian began to relax. Gradually, as the evening progressed, she was able to stop holding her breath whenever the subject was changed, afraid that Stephanie's name might come up in the conversation.

The dinner was excellent, the wine served with it of the best although Gillian noticed that Owen drank only orange juice, aware he would have to drive the Range Rover back to the cottage through the snow. Gillian enjoyed a glass of wine but even she drank sparingly.

The topics of conversation covered throughout the meal were light and amusing. Owen had tales to tell about people he had met through his life as an antique dealer and Dan, too, turned out to be quite a raconteur. Neither of the Palmers put any sort of pressure on Gillian, asking her no awkward questions about herself that she would not, of course, have been able to answer.

After the meal, they all returned to the drawing-room for coffee in front of the blazing fire. Owen sat close to Gillian and took hold of her hand to squeeze her fingers gently. She smiled at him, feeling a warm glow that had nothing to do with the heat of the fire.

This is my fiancé, she thought. It was not an unpleasant notion. She wondered idly what Dr Morgan would have to say on her next visit when she told him she was engaged to be married to someone she could not remember.

Diana got up presently to take the coffee tray into the kitchen. Gillian rose as well.

'May I help you in any way?' she asked.

Diana waved the offer aside kindly.

'No, no, I'll just stack the dishwasher. It won't take me more than a few minutes.'

Gillian asked where the bathroom was and Diana directed her to the cloakroom in the hall which was opposite the kitchen. When she came out a few moments later, the kitchen was in darkness but there was a light showing through the open doorway of a room just before the drawing-room. Gillian had to pass this room and as she did, she heard Diana calling out her name. She hesitated in the doorway. Diana was standing by a large desk. It was a small room, lined with books, a study of some sort. Gillian could see at once that Diana had been crying. She moved a few steps into the room.

'Is something wrong?' she asked.

Diana gave her a tremulous smile. She was holding something in her hand, and Gillian saw that it was a small photograph frame.

'No, I'm all right,' Owen's mother said. 'I was just looking at this.'

She glanced back at the photograph.

'I told Dan to put away all the photographs because I couldn't bear to look at them, but he either missed this one or kept it out anyway. He worships her,' she explained.

Gillian didn't know what to say but Diana went on.

'I pray every night that she's safe and well somewhere but I do worry about her.'

'You're talking about Stephanie, aren't you?' Gillian asked quietly.

Diana nodded.

'Yes. Has Owen told you about her?'

'A little.'

So the subject Gillian had wished to avoid was being mentioned after all.

'She's so young, such a child. And she's not well. Why doesn't she phone us, Gillian, and let us know where she is? That's all I ask.'

Was it really all she asked, Gillian wondered. She had a feeling that if and when Stephanie came home, her parents would intend to keep a very close eye on her in future.

'I'm sure you'll hear from her before long,' she said with more confidence than she was feeling.

A look of hope flashed in Diana's eyes but only for a brief moment.

'I wish I could believe that,' she said with a sigh.

She came round the side of the desk, holding out the small photograph frame.

'Stephanie's very beautiful. Look at her, Gillian.'

Politely Gillian took hold of the picture, but as she glanced at it, her heart gave a sudden wild lurch, the blood seemed to drain out of her head and for one dreadful minute she thought she was going to faint. She steadied herself against the desk.

'Are you all right, dear?' Diana asked anxiously.

Gillian carefully put the photograph frame back on the desk, turning the picture away from herself so that she wouldn't have to see that beautiful, sad-looking face staring out at her.

'No, I suddenly don't feel well,' she stammered.

'Oh, dear, I'm so sorry. Would you like a glass of water perhaps?'

'Perhaps Owen should take me home,' Gillian suggested.

She couldn't describe how she felt, not at that moment. She had to understand what was going on in her head. It was as though there was a camera in there, taking random snaps, lighting up dark corners, showing her glimpses she wasn't sure she wanted to see.

Diana took her back into the drawing-room. As soon as Owen saw her he rushed over to her.

'Gillian, are you sick?' he asked anxiously.

Diana answered for her.

'She almost fainted a minute ago. You'd better take her home, Owen. Perhaps she's over-tired. After all, she is just recovering from an accident, you know.'

'Yes, of course,' Owen said quickly.

'I'll get your coats,' Dan said, leaving the room.

Gillian was shaking.

'I think she's got a touch of flu,' Diana said, seeing her involuntary shudders.

Gillian almost laughed. It certainly wasn't flu, and she wasn't sick, except in her head. But she had to get away, to sort out what was happening to her. Once out in the cold, crisp night air she felt slightly better. She fastened her seat belt and stared through the windscreen, all without saying a word to Owen.

Before he started up the car he said, 'Will you be all right, darling?'

'Yes. Just take me home.'

Gillian couldn't look at him. She wanted to explain but the words wouldn't come. She stared at the headlight beams of the Range Rover lighting up the snowy road ahead. Snow still clung to the bare, black branches of trees and bushes, but Gillian saw none of it. The camera inside her head stopped whirring and the kaleidoscope of images began to steady and to clarify.

Slowly, she began to remember . . .

CHAPTER SEVEN

It was already getting dark when Gillian left Owen's cottage that fateful day. He walked her to her car, staring anxiously at the sky.

'It might start to snow,' he said. 'Won't you please stay the night and travel back in the morning?'

'Sorry, darling, I can't,' Gillian said. 'I've got two parties this week.'

Owen smiled indulgently.

'Yes, I know, the show must go on.'

Gillian gave his shoulder a mock punch.

'Yes, it must,' she chided him. 'Don't worry, I'll be all right. I'm used to driving in the dark.'

He kissed her and she fastened her arms around his neck.

'Thank you for saying you'll marry me,' Owen whispered lovingly.

'Thank you for asking me,' Gillian returned.

She looked at the ring on her left hand.

'It's so beautiful, Owen, but you took me completely by surprise, you know. I had no idea you were going to ask me to marry you.'

'I was missing you so terribly and I suddenly decided I wanted to spend the rest of my life with you.'

They stood locked in a close embrace for several moments. Then Gillian broke away.

'Well, I suppose I'd better be off.'

'Drive carefully, do you hear me? And phone me when you get home.'

'I will, I promise.'

'And I'll come down as soon as I can, that's a promise, too.'

Gillian gave a little frown.

'Can't you tell me what's wrong that's forced you to move up here, Owen? After all, I shall be your wife one day.'

'The sooner the better,' Owen said fervently. 'But, bear with me, darling. It's not that I'm trying to shut you out, its just that I promised Mother.'

'Of course. I understand.'

But Gillian didn't really know if she understood at all. Owen seemed to be deliberately keeping something from her and it troubled her. She knew that his parents lived fairly close by and had imagined she would be meeting them once Owen had asked her to marry him, but she had not done so. She knew there was something wrong. Why else had Owen left Bourton-on-the-Water so quickly?

But, she thought as she glanced at the beautiful ring Owen had placed on her finger only that afternoon, she would trust him implicitly. He would tell her everything when he was able to, she was sure of that. She got in the car and Owen bent to give her one last kiss.

'God speed, Gillian,' he said.

'Thank you. Look at all those stars. It's a

lovely night. It won't snow tonight.'

Gillian's voice was confident, but Owen just smiled and wiggled his fingers at her and Gillian closed the window, shutting out the bitter cold of the darkening afternoon. Well, she had a long drive ahead of her but she didn't mind. She liked driving and she knew she was a good driver.

She had the knowledge, too, that Owen loved her and that she loved him. That would keep her warm, and she had the radio for company and the thought of a warm bed waiting to comfort her.

She had left Helmsley behind and was driving along a fairly narrow country road before she met the main road when her headlights picked out a figure walking along the road ahead of her, a slender, hunched figure in dark clothing. As she got nearer, Gillian could see that the figure had a large backpack on its back, hands deep in coat pockets.

It wasn't so late but Gillian felt a twinge of concern when she realised it was a young woman walking alone in the dark of a very cold night. She felt she couldn't simply drive past without offering a lift, so she pulled into the side of the road a few yards past the walking figure and wound down the window.

'Going far?' she asked.

The girl bent down. She was wearing a woolly hat pulled well over her ears but Gillian could see that she had a startlingly beautiful face with enormous dark eyes.

'Yes, I'm afraid I am.'

She spoke cheerfully.

'On foot at night in February?' Gillian queried.

'Needs must.'

The girl shrugged her shoulders. Gillian could tell that she was feeling the weight of the heavy backpack.

'I was hoping to gain the main road and then hitch a lift south,' she said.

'How far south?'

'Where are you headed?'

'Gloucestershire. Would a lift from me be any good to you?'

The girl grinned.

'Would it? I'm grateful for anything, but as it happens I'm bound for Bath, for the university there, so your coming along is very fortuitous for me.'

Gillian opened the door.

'Jump in,' she offered. 'Let me put your bag in the boot.'

Soon they were on their way again. The girl pulled off her hat and ran her fingers through her short, dark hair.

'Oh, my, what bliss,' she said, leaning her head back and closing her eyes. 'The warmth I mean. It's freezing out there.'

Gillian glanced at her.

'And do you mean to tell me you're actually

hitchhiking back to university?'

The girl turned solemn eyes on her.

'It's a long story,' she said. 'Please, don't ask me to explain. I'm very grateful to you and I promise I'm not a highway robber or anything like that. I don't want to pinch your car, but don't ask me why I'm travelling in such an unorthodox and foolhardy fashion. All right?'

She had a disarming way with her and Gillian felt it wasn't really any of her business. She didn't feel threatened in any way and was only glad that she had been in the right place at the right time.

'My name's Gillian,' she introduced herself.

'Stephanie,' the girl replied.

There was silence for a few moments. Gillian realised how nice it felt to have someone in the car with her.

'Do you live in Gloucestershire?' Stephanie queried.

'Yes, I do, in Bourton-on-the-Water. I've just been visiting my fiancé. Actually we just got engaged today.'

'Congratulations. Oh, yes, I can see your ring. Very nice.'

Gillian gave her a sidelong glance.

'Of course, perhaps I shouldn't tell you anything about myself either.'

'Touché,' Stephanie said with a cheeky smile. 'All right, if you must know, I've just bust up with my boyfriend. We were supposed to be travelling back to Bath together tomorrow or the day after, but being the headstrong creature I am I decided to go it alone. We're both locals, you see, and have been home for a long weekend.'

'Won't your boyfriend worry about you?' Gillian asked.

'I guess he will. Serves him right if he does, but I'll phone him from a service station when we're on the motorway. You will be stopping, I take it?'

'Yes, I suppose so.'

Gillian could see that Stephanie was a young lady of great confidence and spirit.

'Good, that's fine. And where does your fiancé live, Gillian?'

Stephanie's voice was interested and chatty.

Gillian didn't mind talking about Owen, about how they met, she was happy to do so and Stephanie proved to be a very good listener. So much so that Gillian talked at some length, not only about Owen and their future plans but about her life in general, her work and her home. She even found she could talk about her sister, Carol, and this was something she hadn't been able to do for some time.

She had told Owen only the barest details about Carol. Now, to a complete stranger, the words seemed to come easily and had a curious therapeutic effect on her, so that by the time they stopped at a motorway service station for something to eat, she felt as though she and Stephanie had known one another for ages.

Whilst Gillian sipped a piping hot chocolate drink, and finished her buttered toast, Stephanie went off to find a phone, but only on Gillian's insistence.

'If you don't,' Gillian warned, 'I shall leave you here to hitch another ride.'

Stephanie looked as though she didn't believe a word of that threat but went off happily enough. She came back with a smile on her face.

'We've kissed and made up,' she said, 'or as much as we were able to do over the phone. Of course, he's livid with me for going off the way I did, but I've told him that's the way I am and he'll have to get used to it.'

This sounded rather selfish and thoughtless to Gillian but she didn't say so. Stephanie sat down to finish her milkshake. As she did so she glanced across at the windows.

'Oh, my goodness,' she cried, 'it's started to snow.'

Gillian looked across as well.

'Owen said it might. Ah, well, there's no problem, I suppose, whilst we're on the motorways. But I don't think you'll make it to Bath tonight, Stephanie. Would you like to stop off at my place and then you'll probably be able to use a more regular form of transport tomorrow? Er . . . do you have any money?'

'A bit,' was all Stephanie said. 'Gosh, it's very nice of you, Gillian, to offer me a bed for the night and I'll accept with grateful thanks. It was certainly my lucky day to have met you.'

The snow was coming down very heavily when they left the service station and Gillian had to keep the wipers moving fast. Even so, the snow flakes seemed to build up and despite the fairly fast-moving traffic the motorway had a fine covering of snow, with surrounding fields and hills soon becoming a winter wonderland.

Gillian wondered what sort of problems they would encounter when they left the motorway. There were some country roads to negotiate before they reached Bourton. She would just have to keep her fingers crossed. She didn't communicate her worries to Stephanie who seemed totally unconcerned about the worsening weather. She fiddled with the radio and then spotted the handful of cassettes that Gillian kept in the car.

'Can I try one of these?' she asked.

'Go ahead,' Gillian said, not taking her eyes off the road.

It was going to take her longer than she had estimated to reach home because she now had to drive really slowly. She hoped Owen wouldn't start to worry about her, especially if he watched the TV news and the snow was reported.

Stephanie wasn't too impressed by Gillian's

choice of music and before long had switched off the cassette player and sat silently, for once, staring through the windscreen. It seemed to suit them both not to talk for a while. They had left the motorway at last and now came the trickiest part of the journey home, through narrow, winding roads where the snow had begun to build up and visibility through the flakes was very poor.

When Gillian realised the car was beginning to skid and that she was having great difficulty controlling it, she began to panic. She forced herself to try to remain calm. She had to keep going. If she stopped now she would never get the car started again and they would be stuck in a drift for goodness knew how long. They seemed to be the only ones on the road.

Occasionally they passed a house or a cluster of houses with bright, comforting lights burning and Gillian envied the occupants sitting in the warmth, safe and secure. She was aware of how tense she was and Stephanie, too, seemed hunched up in her seat, her eyes fixed steadily on the windscreen wipers as though mesmerised by their movement.

When Stephanie suddenly said, 'How much farther have we to go, Gillian?' Gillian could detect the nervousness in her voice.

She momentarily took her eyes off the road ahead to smile with a confidence she was far from feeling.

'Oh, not long and I've left the central

heating on and a fire just ready to light.'

'Sounds wonderful,' Stephanie sighed.

Then the car gave an almighty lurch, twisting to one side of the road and then the other so rapidly that Gillian knew she was losing control. She saw the tree just before they hit it and everything went black . . .

CHAPTER EIGHT

Owen helped her out of the Range Rover once back at his cottage, and opened the door. They went inside together. Gillian felt unable to talk to him though she knew he was desperately concerned about her. Gathering her courage in both hands Gillian turned to Owen.

'I've got to go home tonight,' she said.

'But you can't!' he protested.

For answer Gillian went and rested her head against him and he put his arms around her and held her close. Her thoughts were all over the place with all she was now remembering.

'What's wrong, Gillian? Something's upset you? Was it mother?'

'In a way, yes,' Gillian said without moving from the haven of Owen's arms. 'But she didn't mean to. She couldn't possibly have known.'

'Known what?'

Gillian looked into his serious dark eyes.

'I can't tell you that yet. Do you remember when you came back to Helmsley to live you told me to be patient with you when I wanted to know the reason you'd left Bourton? Well, it's like that with me now. Please, trust me, Owen. There's something I have to do.'

'Of course I trust you, but . . .'

Then Owen broke off and stared at her, holding her at arms' length.

'But that conversation was before you lost your memory, wasn't it?'

Gillian smiled.

'Yes, it was, and now I remember.'

Owen looked delighted.

'Darling, that's wonderful! When? How? Do you remember everything?'

'Not everything.'

It was true, some things were still vague and shrouded. She had been able to recall Carol but now her sister had slipped back into the darkness again and no matter how she tried to get her head round her thoughts she couldn't get her sister back. She only knew that Carol and Stephanie were connected and she had to get home and wait for Stephanie to return from Stratford so that she could find out the truth. Oh, she knew she might be able to find out from Owen but at this stage she didn't want to involve him. There was too much to clear up in her own mind first.

Only when she felt capable of dealing with her own emotions could she possibly tell him that she knew where his sister was. All she knew for certain was that she had picked up a young girl on the road that night, a girl who had obviously told her a tissue of lies. In fact the only truth Stephanie had ever told her was her name and that only at the start of their acquaintance.

The knowledge that Owen's sister had been living in her home, pretending to be her own sister, scared her. Where was the real Carol? And there were other more sinister facts to consider. Stephanie had not only lied, she had behaved in a devious and underhand manner. Gillian needed to know why before she burdened Owen and his parents with the knowledge that she knew where Stephanie was. She didn't mean to be cruel. She knew how desperate they must be for news of Stephanie, but a few more days wasn't going to hurt them, and this was the only way she could deal with things. It had to be her way, in her time.

'But you do remember me? Us?' Owen asked.

Gillian kissed him on the lips.

'Yes, that I do remember. Oh, Owen, it feels so wonderful!'

They kissed for a long time. Then Owen held up Gillian's left hand.

'Perhaps you remember what you did with your ring. Did you lose it in the accident?'

'I don't think so.'

Gillian was hesitant. She knew exactly what had happened to the ring. Stephanie had it. Stephanie was shrewd and cunning. She had gone out of her way to ensure Gillian didn't know she had a fiancé. The reason wasn't exactly clear at the moment but it would be, along with other things, and if Gillian had her way, before she was very much older! That's why she had to return to Bourton tonight no matter how late it was. She would drive all night if necessary. She would be prepared to risk it snowing again and this time she would not be picking up any lonely strangers along the way!

When Owen started to speak Gillian put her fingers gently against his lips.

'Darling, let me go,' she pleaded. 'I have to do this. I'll phone you as soon as I can, I promise.'

'I don't want you to go, Gillian.'

Owen sounded really worried.

'Not tonight. Last time I let you drive off alone into the night you got hurt. How can I put you at risk like that again?'

'Because you don't have any choice,' Gillian told him. 'And this time, I promise you, I shan't get hurt. I've remembered everything about us, Owen. How we met, the first time we kissed. I've remembered how very much I love you and I'm ready to marry you as soon as it's humanly possible, but you have to let me go and with your blessing.'

She looked at him and she could see he was trying to think of something to say, but he couldn't find the words and he simply crushed her against him, stroking her hair.

'Darling, darling Gillian. You're beautiful and headstrong and stubborn and I love you. If you weren't all those things you wouldn't be you and I shouldn't love you the way that I do,' he whispered.

Beautiful words that made Gillian's heart swell with love for him, too. She prayed there would be a speedy resolve to their mystery.

*   *   *

Gillian half expected to see a welcoming light beaming from the cottage, a light which would indicate that Carol, no, Stephanie, was back from Stratford, but everything was in total darkness, though the exterior security light came on as she drove into the driveway. She felt relief that Stephanie wasn't there. She wasn't yet ready to face the girl who had pretended to be her sister.

On the drive down, she had gone over and over in her mind the events leading up to the accident and what had followed, and she had come to the conclusion that Stephanie had taken on Carol's identity as soon as she had discovered that Gillian had no memory of the events of their meeting, or indeed of any part of her life. It had taken a certain kind of cunning and guile to be able to do this, not to say a strong nerve. Did she really think she could get away with it for ever? Stephanie had certainly taken on board everything that Gillian had told her to know so many facts about, not only Gillian's life, but Carol's, too.

Carol, her sister, was like a ghost hovering

in the background and Gillian had a cold, empty feeling when she tried to recall her, as though there was something to fear about knowing the truth about her.

As soon as she had parked in front of the garage, she hurried indoors. She went into the kitchen to put on the kettle, then lowered the blinds and drew the curtains in the other rooms to shut out the inky blackness outside. Then she turned up the heating. She hovered by the telephone. Should she phone Owen to let him know she was home? Quickly she decided not to. She needed to know more about Stephanie, and more about Carol before she spoke to Owen.

After drinking a mug of hot chocolate and munching a couple of biscuits Gillian decided there was no time like the present to get down to it. She had no idea when Stephanie would be back. It could be at any time. First, she had to search Stephanie's bedroom to see if she could find the engagement ring that Owen had given her. She had no doubt in her mind that Stephanie had removed the ring and hidden it away and the reason seemed obvious.

If Gillian had realised from the ring that she was engaged to be married she would naturally have wanted to know who her fiancé was. Stephanie, of course, would not want that. Owen was her brother and she had run away from home. She couldn't possibly risk a link up between him and Gillian.

For the same reason, Gillian was sure Stephanie had torn the page from her diary. And she must not forget that Carol's picture had disappeared after she herself had made remarks about how Carol's looks had changed.

Searching through the drawers and cupboards in the bedroom Gillian came to another conclusion. On her earlier attempt to tidy the room the odd variance of clothes had puzzled her. Faded jeans alongside smart, woollen trousers; well-washed sweaters with designer knitwear. Now she was vividly recalling how Stephanie always dressed. She was the one with the good clothes. Carol had placed far less importance on what she wore. Carol had gone to Rumania to do charity work. Her wardrobe seemed to fit in with her lifestyle.

'Carol, oh, Carol.'

Gillian spoke her name out loud. Why couldn't she remember her sister, the most important thing of all?

A thorough search of the bedroom revealed nothing. Gillian sat on the edge of the bed, unsure what she could do next. Where else could she look? Did Stephanie have the ring with her? She wandered into the living-room which was now quite warm, and sat on the couch staring at the fireplace with its arrangements of logs just waiting for a match to be put to the paper and firelighters.

Owen sprang into her mind, darling Owen.

How lucky she was to have found such a wonderful man. She must phone him. As she went towards her desk in a corner of the room Gillian remembered the locked drawer without a key. She was convinced she had not locked the drawer so it must follow that Stephanie had done so and if so, there had to be a reason. Gillian knew it was useless to try to find a key but she could attempt to force the drawer open.

She went into the kitchen and found a sturdy, flat-bladed knife. Even if she caused damage to the desk she had no course but to get that top drawer open by any means she could! It wasn't easy but eventually the lock gave and she was able to pull the drawer open. And there it was! A diamond solitaire ring wrapped in tissue paper.

It was like seeing an old friend because Gillian had seen the ring in her mind whilst re-living that fateful trip from Yorkshire. She slipped it on her finger. It was a perfect fit as she had known it would be. Tears sprang to her eyes and she wiped them away with the back of her hand.

How could Stephanie do that to her? Gillian felt hurt and upset that someone she had helped, had planned to offer shelter for the night to, could act in such a malicious fashion. But the discovery of the ring was only the start of her pain and misery. On top of the contents of the drawer was the picture of

Carol that had stood on the mantelpiece. There had been no accident. The glass had never been broken. Stephanie had removed the picture, locked it away in the drawer, so that Gillian wouldn't see it every day and study it and maybe begin to ask awkward questions.

Under the picture was a manilla folder made of stiff cardboard with an overlap and a piece of white band tied around it. Gillian's fingers trembled as she untied the ribbon and opened up the file. At first there was nothing obvious to alarm her—insurance certificates for the bungalow and the contents; some ancient swimming certificates that she and Carol had received whilst at school; even old report cards; items of that nature, sentimental reminders of a happy past.

As Gillian looked through them she felt her heart quicken. She was remembering so vividly the day Carol left for Rumania, the way they had clung to one another in tears.

'Don't worry about me, Gillian, I'll be fine. Dr Marsden and his wife will take good care of me,' Carol had said.

The good doctor had called for Carol, driving a lorry which was laden with goods of every sort, food, clothes, bandages, medicines, donated and collected by many other good people.

Carol's last words were, 'I'll be home before you know it,' but she hadn't come home, and there in front of Gillian, seen through eyes blinded by tears, was Dr Marsden's letter.

I'm so very sorry to have to inform you, the letter said, *that Carol died yesterday. She caught some virus, God knows what, and there was nothing anyone could do about it. I'm a doctor, but I was helpless, Gillian. It was over in a matter of hours. I wanted to phone you but phoning from here at present is practically impossible, especially where we are. But a colleague of mine had managed to contact the British Consulate and I'm sure they'll be in touch with you. I'm so very, very sorry, Gillian. I cannot find the words to tell you just how sorry I am.*

There had been more. Arrangements had to be made for a funeral. Did she want Carol's body bringing home? Of course she did. There was the ceremony itself, the packed crematorium, the flowers, the glowing tributes. And afterwards, when it all began to sink in, the despair, the loneliness, the bitter grieving. And then, Gillian had met Owen and had slowly learned to smile again.

She had told him about Carol's death, but even with Owen she had been unable to really unburden her grief. How ironic it was that with a stranger she had picked up one snowy night she had at last been able to talk freely about Carol and her death and had been totally unaware that the sharing of such confidences would be turned against her in the way that it had.

With the letter she found Carol's death certificate and both their birth certificates, together with the death certificates of their parents. Had Stephanie's hands rifled through these most personal and precious possessions or had she merely gone into the drawer for a safe hiding place for the ring and photograph?

The shrill noise of the telephone made Gillian jump up with a start. She grabbed the receiver.

'Hello,' she gasped.

'Gillian, it's me.'

'Owen!'

Oh, how she wished just then that he was there so she could weep in his arms and have him comfort her.

'How are you, darling? Was the journey very bad?'

'No, no, not bad at all. No snow to speak of most of the way down, none at all here in Bourton.'

'That's good.' Owen sounded relieved. 'I expect you're tired.'

'Very.'

She ached with fatigue but she knew she would not be able to sleep well that night and she had a worse ordeal yet to face, when Stephanie finally came back.

'I'll let you get to bed then. I'm coming down there as soon as I can, Gillian. Mother and Dad will just have to cope on their own for a while. I don't intend to be parted from you for much longer.'

She must tell him. She couldn't let him ring off without telling him something at least.

'Owen,' she began, 'oh, I don't know how to put this.'

'What's the matter?' Owen said, then went on. 'Have you been crying, Gillian?'

'Owen, I know where Stephanie is.'

'You know? But how can you know?'

'I just do. She's in Stratford at the moment, but she's been living here with me in Bourton. No, don't interrupt, Owen, let me try to explain. It's a long story. When my memory came back to me it was because your mother had showed me a picture of Stephanie and I recognised her and suddenly my mind started to clear.'

'I don't think I follow you,' Owen said quietly.

'That night in February, after we got engaged, I picked up a hitchhiker soon after I left Helmsley. She told me she was going back to Bath University and I agreed to give her a lift at least part of the way. She told me a lot of lies, as I know now, Owen, but in one respect she told me the truth. She said her name was Stephanie.'

'You mean to say when Stephanie left home you took her in your car all the way to Gloucestershire and she's been there ever since?'

'Yes, but can't you see, it's not as

straightforward as it seems. We had the accident that night and I couldn't remember who I was or anything about myself. But Stephanie was there at my side when I came round. She helped me pick up the pieces. The only thing is, she told me she was my sister. She said she was Carol.'

'Carol? But, Gillian, Carol's dead.'

'I know, I know that now.'

Gillian had started to cry again.

'I had told Stephanie all about Carol. I told her a great deal and she capitalised on what I told her and took Carol's place. Oh, Owen, I'm so confused. Stephanie will be back any day now. What am I going to say to her?'

'I'm coming down, Gillian.'

Owen's voice was grim.

'I'll go and see my parents first thing in the morning and then I'll leave right away. I can hardly believe what you've just told me. It seems so far-fetched.'

'It's the truth, Owen.'

'Oh, I'm not doubting your word, but what induced Stephanie to do such a terrible thing? What should I tell Mum and Dad?'

'Don't tell them anything yet,' Gillian suggested. 'just tell them you're coming to see me. Tell them I've regained my memory and we want to spend some time together. Let's wait till you can see Stephanie and talk to her before you put more worry on your parents' shoulders.'

'Yes, you're right. Are you sure you can manage tonight, darling? I'll be there as soon as I can.'

Gillian felt better already for having spoken to Owen.

'I'll be fine,' she told him.

He told her he loved her and they said good-night. Gillian carefully replaced the file of papers and documents in the drawer and sat on the couch for some time thinking about the events of that evening. Everything had moved so quickly, leaving her with a spinning head, but she took comfort from the fact that tomorrow Owen would be there. And this time, she promised herself, she was not going to let him out of her sight ever again!

CHAPTER NINE

The next morning brought promise of a lovely day, with a slight breeze, plenty of sunshine and through the sitting-room window Gillian could see that there were fresh green shoots appearing on trees and bushes. Spring would soon be here, a time of hope, a time of renewal. Would it prove to be so for her and Owen? And Stephanie?

Gillian wondered how she was going to get through the time till Stephanie came back. The only thing that sustained her was knowing Owen would be there later in the day. She tried to keep busy throughout the morning, doing some washing, cleaning the house, checking her appointments diary, writing some letters. She sat at the desk, noting the damaged drawer which would need repairing. Perhaps Owen would see to that.

The answering machine sat next to the telephone. Gillian wondered if she should check it for any sign of Owen's messages which he had left at the time of her accident, but then decided it wouldn't do any good. She was convinced Stephanie had cleared the tape. Gillian knew she herself had already been through her messages and there was definitely nothing from Owen. She pulled her small, portable typewriter towards her to begin the letters.

When her correspondence was finished she stamped all the envelopes and left them ready for posting. It was now almost noon. What time would Owen arrive? Should she wait for him before she made any lunch? She decided not to wait and was looking in the fridge for something suitable to eat when a shadow passed the kitchen window. Goodness, was Owen here already? But no, it wasn't Owen who walked breezily into the house—it was Stephanie, looking pink-cheeked, alert, healthy with the inevitable woollen hat pulled over her hair.

Gillian felt her heart skip a beat. She was now faced with a confrontation for which she was not really prepared.

'Hello,' she greeted, leaving out any name.

Stephanie smiled.

'Hi!'

She took off her coat and went to hang it in the hallrobe. Then she came back into the kitchen, minus her small suitcase and hat, her short hair spiky where she had pushed her fingers through it, a gesture she regularly performed when removing her hat.

'Oh, I've had such a lovely time. Been to the theatre, of course, dined out. The hotel was wonderful. I can't thank you enough, Gillian, for giving me that money. Without your help it would have been practically impossible for me to pay my way. Have you had your lunch yet?

I'm starving.'

'Not yet,' Gillian said quietly. 'I thought I might make an omelette. We don't seem to have much else but eggs in at the moment.'

She hoped and prayed that Owen wouldn't arrive just then. She needed to speak to Stephanie alone before that happened. Stephanie's eyebrows rose.

'What, you've allowed the cupboard to get bare?' she teased. 'Shame on you!'

Gillian couldn't bring herself to smile. She wasn't so much of a hypocrite. She went to fill the kettle and to get a bowl for the eggs. Stephanie sat on a corner of the table, watching her, talking non-stop.

'I might be having someone round for a meal before long, Gillian. Will that be all right?'

'Someone you met in Stratford?' Gillian asked without looking round.

'No, he went with us.'

'He?'

Gillian knew she sounded surprised.

'You'll like him.'

Stephanie came and leaned against the worktop, watching Gillian beating the eggs.

'His name is David. He's twenty-three, the same age as I am.'

Then Gillian did turn to look at Stephanie and the words were out before she could stop them.

'But you're not twenty-three, are you?

94

You're nineteen. I always thought you looked very young for your age. Now I know why.'

Stephanie's eyes opened very wide and all the healthy pinkness seemed to drain out of her face.

'What on earth are you talking about, Gillian?' she said.

'I'm talking about you, Stephanie. Oh, yes, you ought to look horrified. I know who you are. You're Owen Palmer's sister, and Owen is my fiancé. You see, I've remembered, everything!'

Stephanie backed away and sat down at the table. She looked stunned and for once was speechless as Gillian went on.

'How could you do it, Stephanie? How could you be so cruel, so malicious, so deceitful?'

At last, Stephanie found her voice but her brightness had deserted her. She had taken on a wary look, her dark eyes narrowed, her fingers clutching at each other in her lap.

'When . . . when did you remember? What made you remember?'

'Seeing your photograph. That was the start of it.'

'My photograph? There's no photograph of me in this house.'

'I know there isn't, but there's one of Carol, isn't there? The one you said was you. The one you said you'd broken the glass of and were having it replaced. Just one of the many lies you told me, Stephanie.'

'I couldn't help it. I was desperate.'

Stephanie was now wildly trying to defend her indefensible actions.

'When you gave me that lift I had to lie to you, to give you a believable reason for my being on the road that night. Then, after the crash, when you regained consciousness the first time, and I realised you couldn't remember who you were, or who I was, or anything about yourself, I decided your amnesia was a stroke of luck for me. You'd told me so much about yourself and about Carol, it seemed so easy to tell the doctor at the hospital that I was your sister. I knew he wouldn't know your sister was dead. I got your keys from your bag and came here and acquainted myself with everything about your home. I had a few days' grace. I even got myself a part-time job at the charity shop. I knew it wouldn't be safe to lie about that in case you ever went in there.'

'And that's not all you did, is it, Stephanie?'

Gillian felt angry and bitterly hurt inside, but kept her emotions under control.

'You took my ring, the one Owen had given me, and you tore the page out of my diary so I wouldn't find his name and address. But I did find it, because I was suspicious when I found the page missing. Of course, never in my wildest dreams could I have guessed what you'd done. You even fooled me about the broken picture glass.'

'But you know everything now, don't you?' Stephanie asked.

'Yes, everything! I found the torn diary page and I went to Helmsley, to Owen's house, and I discovered not only that he knew me but that we were engaged to be married, something I'd told you, hadn't I, the night I picked you up? Then I met your parents and they told me how upset they were because you'd run away from home. Owen told me you went missing on the very night I was up there. He told me all about you, Stephanie, but at that time, of course, I had no idea you and I had met. That came later when your mother showed me your picture. That's when I started to remember. I came back here then. I didn't tell Owen the truth. I couldn't.'

A tiny gleam of hope seemed to come into Stephanie's eyes.

'So Owen doesn't know I'm here? He doesn't know what I've done?'

'Oh, yes, he does,' Gillian told her and couldn't quite keep the note of triumph out of her voice. 'He rang me last night and I told him everything, because by that time I'd found my ring and Carol's photograph, in the locked drawer. And I'd found Dr Marsden's letter and Carol's death certificate. I remembered it all then. My past, the grief I felt when Carol died, so when Owen phoned it was such a relief to share my burden with him. He's coming down here, today.'

Stephanie leaped to her feet.

'When?' she demanded.

'I don't know. As soon as he can.'

'You shouldn't have let him, Gillian. I don't want him here.'

Stephanie was yelling now, almost beside herself.

'He'll take me back home, and they'll make me see another doctor. I don't need to see doctors. There's nothing wrong with me. Do you know something? For the first time in ages I was really beginning to enjoy my life. I was free. I had some real friends, people who cared for me, not like John Lawton, who lied to me and cheated me and treated me like dirt.'

'As you've done with me, wouldn't you say?' Gillian said quietly.

Stephanie's tirade seemed to cease as quickly as it had begun.

'I'm sorry, Gillian, I'm truly sorry, you must believe me. I felt cornered and then I saw a means of escape. I saw it was possible for me to be safe, at least for a while. Oh, I knew there was always the possibility that your memory would return. In fact, I knew it was inevitable, but I was willing to take that risk because I didn't have any choice. But now, it's finished for me. Owen will be furious and he'll think I'm psychotic. They'll lock me away.'

'Of course they won't. But, Stephanie, how

can you explain what you did? Was it the action of a well-balanced person?'

'I've told you, I've told you!'

The anger was back.

'I felt like a cornered animal, my every move watched. I was never allowed any freedom. That's why I started seeing John Lawton in the first place, to get back at my parents for the way they treated me. Then . . . then John . . .'

She burst into tears, sitting down again, her face buried in her hands. She looked so young, so vulnerable, with her shoulders shaking and great sobs coming from her that Gillian was overcome with emotion herself. She went and put her arms around Stephanie's bent shoulders.

'Stephanie, don't cry, you'll make yourself ill,' she said kindly. 'I'm sure you're wrong about Owen. He's the kindest, most wonderful person.'

'To you maybe, not to me!' Stephanie shot at her.

She jumped to her feet again and gave Gillian a hard push, sending her reeling back against the sink.

'He'll talk you round and you'll begin to think like he does. Oh, leave me alone. You don't understand!'

She dashed out of the kitchen and a moment later Gillian heard the bedroom door slam loudly. She didn't know what to do.

Should she go after Stephanie, try to comfort her? It was amazing how her own anger had seemed to evaporate with the onset of Stephanie's distress. Of course, Stephanie had behaved badly, even wickedly, but was it true what she said. Did she feel like a trapped animal? Could Owen really be the tyrant she was making him out to be? Or was this yet another facet of Stephanie's many-sided character? A ploy for sympathy? Another act of cunning?

Gillian decided that for the moment she would leave Stephanie to cry alone. She would make some tea then go and see what she could do. They would talk their way through this. And then, perhaps, Owen would be here and when he was Gillian would make sure he didn't do or say anything that would upset Stephanie further. She smiled to herself. From being Stephanie's accuser she was now putting herself in the position of protector.

She turned to the cupboards and started getting down cups and saucers, the tin of biscuits, looking to see if there were any more of the chocolate biscuits which, she knew, were Stephanie's favourites. It was as she was doing this that she heard the sound of a car being started up.

She ran to the window just in time to see her car speeding out of the open gateway and disappearing down the road with a squeal of brakes, and when she ran into the hall she saw that the front door and the door of Stephanie's bedroom were wide open. She cursed herself for her carelessness, for not being more vigilant.

CHAPTER TEN

Gillian ran out of the house at the end of the drive, staring down the road but by then, of course, there was no sign of the car. There was no point in her trying to follow Stephanie. By the time she had got the van out of the garage, Stephanie would be long gone. She could only wait now till Owen arrived.

She was restless and on edge, but she forced herself to eat some toast, though her appetite for an omelette or anything else substantial had vanished along with Stephanie. The time seemed to drag and when at last Gillian heard the approach of a car she let out a great sigh of relief. Then it occurred to her that it might only be Stephanie returning, but it wasn't. It was Owen's Range Rover and Gillian ran out of the house to meet him. She flung herself into his arms the moment he stepped out of the vehicle.

'My, this is nice,' he said in a teasing voice, kissing her forehead, but Gillian wasn't in the mood for banter.

'Owen,' she began, 'Stephanie came home this morning.'

Owen's smile vanished. They walked together into the house.

'Where is she?' he asked. 'That young lady's got a lot of explaining to do.'

'She's gone again, Owen.'

'What do you mean gone? Gone where?'

'I don't know. She made off in my car when my back was turned.'

Gillian took Owen into the sitting-room, urging him to take off his coat, thinking how wonderful he looked, how much she loved him and wanted to kiss him. But all that must wait. Stephanie must be their main priority.

'She must have had a reason for doing that, Gillian,' Owen said.

'Yes, and I suppose I must take responsibility for her actions, though I never dreamed she would do anything like that. She came back full of herself, about the wonderful time she had had in Stratford, about some boy she'd met. I never intended to blurt out what I knew in the way that I did, but she told me the young man was twenty-three and when she said, "The same age as I am," I couldn't let that go, Owen, because, of course, she was still pretending to be Carol. I let her know that I knew her real age and who she was and it all snowballed from there. Everything came out. The ring, the missing page from my diary, Carol's photograph.'

'You're way ahead of me, Gillian,' Owen admitted. 'Slow down a little.'

His voice was kind, understanding and Gillian gave him a grateful look.

'You're not angry with me, are you, Owen?' she asked anxiously.

'Of course I'm not. Why should I be?'

'I thought perhaps you might think it was my fault Stephanie's run off again.'

Owen put his arm around her shoulders.

'Darling, you're no more to blame now than I, or my parents were the first time Stephanie ran away. She's the one to blame. She's selfish, irresponsible, childish.'

Gillian put her fingers against his lips before he could say any more.

'Owen, she was very upset and I must admit I was beginning to feel sorry for her just before she ran off. She was full of apologies about the way she had behaved. She knew, I'm sure, how wrong it was for her to lie to me and to pretend to be Carol.'

'It was unforgivable of her to do something so awful.'

'Owen, the most important thing is finding Stephanie now, making sure she's safe. Is she legally allowed to drive a car by the way?'

'Oh, yes, she has a licence,' Owen said.

'Thank goodness for that,' she murmured.

'Though at the moment she has no car of her own. It scares me to death to say it, Gillian, but my sister is a reckless driver. She's had a couple of bumps and last time it happened, my father locked her car away until she could behave more responsibly. I suppose that's why she didn't leave in it that night, though come to think of it, there had been an attempt to break into the garage which we put down to a would-be car thief. That must have been Stephanie's handiwork. And what was it you were saying about a ring and a photograph? Are you talking about the engagement ring I gave you, Gillian?'

Gillian told Owen what Stephanie had done. When it looked as though he might explode into anger she held up her left hand.

'I've got it back, and I want to thank you for the ring again, Owen, and to renew my promise to marry you.'

Owen's face softened and they kissed.

'Darling, Gillian,' he murmured.

She told him then about the missing diary page, the photograph of Carol that had mysteriously disappeared and the lack of his messages on the answering machine.

'My sister has spun quite an intricate little web for herself, hasn't she?' Owen said when Gillian had finished.

Gillian considered her next words carefully before she spoke.

'Stephanie said she had no choice but to act like she did. She told me she felt like a cornered animal.'

'A what?' Owen exclaimed.

'Those were the words she used, Owen.'

'What on earth did she mean by that, for goodness' sake?'

'She said she was never allowed any freedom, that someone, either your parents or you, I should imagine, was always watching her. That's why, at the first opportunity she had, she got involved with an older, married man, not particularly because she was madly in love with him, but because she wanted to get back at you.'

Gillian was surprised when Owen actually laughed.

'That's complete and utter nonsense!' he said. 'She was besotted with John Lawton. I told you, didn't I, that she'd even bought herself a wedding dress? And believe me, she could wind us all around her little finger, especially me, Gillian!'

Gillian knew he was telling her the truth, because from her own short acquaintance with Stephanie she could well imagine how easy it would be for Owen's sister to get her own way. She would always have a ready answer for everything. Look how quickly she had come up with the story about falling out with a boyfriend and going back to Bath University. Explanations for whatever Gillian had asked her had tripped easily from her lips, and Gillian could not forget the most terrible thing of all, that Stephanie had masqueraded as her dead sister, Carol.

One thing was certain now—both she and Owen needed to put aside their own strong feelings of frustration and anger. Stephanie must be found. She couldn't be given the opportunity to enter into someone else's life and spin another web of lies.

'What are we going to do to try to get Stephanie back?' she asked anxiously.

Owen shrugged his shoulders.

'I haven't the faintest idea,' he admitted, but seeing her expression, he went on, 'Darling, we tried all we could think of to trace her last time and we were miserably unsuccessful. How do we know Stephanie hasn't travelled the length and breadth of the country by now? Remember, she has transport this time. If she was prepared to travel from Yorkshire to Gloucestershire, setting off on foot and hitching a ride, surely she won't hesitate to put as much space as possible between your place and herself.'

Gillian feared that Owen was right. If the Palmers couldn't find Stephanie, and they had employed a private detective, the outlook seemed grim. But then, she told herself, there couldn't possibly be another gullible fool like herself in the offing, or another accident causing someone to lose their memory and leave the way open for Stephanie to step into another person's shoes.

'What about Stephanie's boyfriend?' she asked. 'She said his name was David and I presume he lives locally.'

'Did Stephanie say exactly where?'

'No, she didn't.'

'Then, let's face it, Gillian, he could live anywhere, and I think looking for him would be like looking for a needle in a haystack.'

Gillian looked at her hands.

'So we just sit here and do nothing?'

Owen gave a short laugh.

'Oh, dear, you sound just like my mother,' he groaned.

Gillian managed a faint smile of her own.

'I'm sorry. I know you're right but I feel so helpless. And what about your parents, Owen? We'll have to contact them and put them in the picture. It would be cruel not to do so.'

'Let's just wait a couple of days, darling,' he suggested. 'If I phone Mother today, I know what will happen. She'll be straight down here and, believe me, you don't want that. Let's look on the bright side and assume Stephanie will come back of her own free will. If she does, then no harm done and that will be the time for my parents to know the whole story and that Stephanie is safe.'

'And if she doesn't?'

Owen leaned forward and kissed Gillian's cheek.

'We'll just have to cross that bridge when we come to it.'

Gillian wanted to be hopeful and she knew in a way that Owen was right. There was no point in upsetting Mrs Palmer any further. But she had a dreadful, sinking feeling that Stephanie wouldn't return. Why should she? Surely she wouldn't want to risk having to face the music over her actions. She knew that Owen had been on his way here and that then there would be two of them, Owen and Gillian to face.

Gillian was certain Stephanie would have headed for this David's place, wherever that might be. Probably, even now, she was spinning him some yarn and you could be certain that if she was, it would be a story that would put Stephanie Palmer in a good light and show her to be a person deserving of love and sympathy.

'I think I'll make some coffee,' she said, standing up.

'Good idea,' Owen said, 'and this evening I'm taking you out for a slap-up meal to celebrate our engagement, if you like.'

He took hold of both her hands, looking lovingly into her eyes. Despite her worries over Stephanie, Gillian felt a suffusion of happiness and contentment.

'That will be lovely, Owen,' she said.

'But first I'd better find somewhere to stay the night. Bound to be plenty of bed-and-breakfast places in Bourton.'

Gillian stared at him.

'But, you'll stay here, of course, in Stephanie's, or rather in my spare room.'

'No, I can't do that,' Owen said.

Gillian laughed.

'Owen, no-one will think you're going to compromise my reputation, you know.'

'It isn't that.'

Owen's face was serious.

'It's just if Stephanie comes back unexpectedly, she'll need that room.'

Gillian admired his optimism, wishing hers was as strong.

'Of course, but you can always take the couch. It's very comfortable. To tell you the truth, Owen, I'd prefer to have you in the house.'

A big smile lit Owen's face.

'Then the couch it is,' he said.

CHAPTER ELEVEN

A couple of days went by and there was no news or sign of Stephanie, but Gillian and Owen tried to keep their worries in the background.

Gillian went to see her doctor at the hospital, taking Owen with her. She told the doctor what had occurred, but nothing about Stephanie, and she was given a clean bill of health. She introduced Owen to the doctor who gave them his warmest congratulations and best wishes for their future together.

When they went out into the hospital carpark, Owen said, 'And that's what counts, darling, our future together.'

He took hold of her hand and gave it a fond squeeze, but into Gillian's mind flashed a picture of the sadness and worry she had seen on Mrs Palmer's face the night she was shown the photograph of Stephanie. She knew there was no possibility of her and Owen getting married until Stephanie had been traced.

She indicated nothing of this worry to Owen but it was a chilling thought to imagine that Stephanie may never be traced. Gillian knew Owen's sister was quite capable of setting up a completely new life for herself, and she would probably be a great deal more careful the second time, doing all she could to avoid being found.

She wondered if Mr and Mrs Palmer would never reach the point when they would be willing to involve the police. To Gillian's mind that seemed the only logical course the way things had progressed, but she would never suggest it because she knew even if she could convince Owen and she wasn't sure she could, the Palmers would not hear of it.

However, though Stephanie was never far from both their minds, Gillian and Owen managed to enjoy life, living only from day to day, enjoying the spring sunshine, going for walks, eating out and, of course, Gillian knew she would have to start to concentrate on her work again, contacting old and new clients.

She was busy searching through her recipe books one morning when there was a ring at the front door. She was alone as Owen had gone to see the man who had bought his antique shop from him. They had become friends during the negotiations to sell the shop and Owen felt it was time this friendship was renewed now that he was back in Bourton for a while. Gillian opened the front door to see a strange, young man on the doorstep. She knew she need not worry that she might know this person in some way. She had no fears of that nature any more.

'Good morning,' the young man began, smiling at her in a friendly way.

He didn't look like a door-to-door salesman

and, anyway, he carried no case or clipboard. He was in his early twenties, fair-haired, blue-eyed, wearing jeans and a blue T-shirt. He had a neat, clean appearance. Gillian saw the red car parked on the kerb outside.

'Good morning,' she returned. 'May I help you?'

'My name's David,' he said, 'David Sanderson. Perhaps you've heard my name mentioned.'

David? Gillian's brow creased. Then realisation dawned.

'David!' she cried. 'Stephanie's David?'

'Yes,' he agreed, 'though I knew her as Carol, of course, in the beginning.'

Gillian ushered him inside.

'You know where Stephanie is?' she asked eagerly.

They went into the sitting-room. Gillian gestured for the young man to sit down. He did so, thanking her. She sat opposite him.

'Yes, I do know where she is,' he admitted, 'though at the moment I'm not at liberty to say where. You're Gillian, I presume?'

'Of course.'

Gillian felt a little niggle of annoyance. She did not feel like playing a game of cat and mouse with David Sanderson. She felt she should offer him something, tea or coffee, but said nothing. Time for such courtesies when he'd told her why he was there.

'You must surely know how worried

Stephanie's parents and her brother are about her whereabouts,' Gillian said quietly.

'Yes,' David said, 'but she made me promise and I can't break a promise, can I?'

'Depends on what you promised.'

'I said I wouldn't tell you where she was staying. All I'm prepared to say for the moment is that she's with me, at my place. By the way, so is your car. Are you desperate for its return?'

'Not particularly. I'm far more worried about Stephanie,' Gillian replied very matter of factly.

David smiled again.

'I'm taking good care of her, don't worry,' he said.

Gillian didn't smile.

'I'm quite sure you are, but she belongs with her family, I'm sure you'll agree.'

The smile vanished.

'No, I don't. I love Stephanie. Someday, when all this is in the past, I want to marry her.'

'You haven't mentioned marriage to Stephanie, I hope,' Gillian said sharply. 'Has she told you anything about herself? If she has, you must know that thinking about getting married is the last thing she needs at the moment.'

'I'm not a fool, Miss Avery.'

The use of her formal title let Gillian know in no uncertain terms that David Sanderson was not very pleased.

'I know everything about Stephanie and, believe me, her welfare is my only concern at the moment.'

'What exactly do you know about her, David?' Gillian asked. 'I must tell you that Stephanie is inclined to stretch the truth somewhat. In fact she . . .'

David interrupted.

'I know she tells out-and-out lies. Is that what you were going to say?'

'Well, yes,' Gillian admitted.

'She's told me everything, about the married man she was seeing, about running away and meeting you, about your loss of memory and her pretending to be your sister.'

'When did she tell you the truth?'

'When she arrived at my house the morning she ran away from here. I must admit I was a bit shocked by her revelations. Up to then I had had no reason to doubt she was who she had said she was, Carol Avery, living in Bourton-on-the-Water with her sister, Gillian. She even told me about Rumania.'

He paused then went on softly.

'I'm so sorry about what happened to your sister, Gillian, and even sorrier for the way Stephanie treated you, but neither of us can possibly be as sorry as Stephanie herself is. The thing is, she doesn't know how to put things right. She doesn't want to have to face you, or her family. That's why I'm here. I wanted to see for myself what sort of a person you were. I wanted to know if you could be forgiving and understanding and generous enough in spirit to welcome Stephanie back without any recriminations.'

'And have you made up your mind about me, or do you need more time?' Gillian asked, smiling now.

David smiled, too.

'Well, let's say I consider myself to be a very good judge of character and I like you, Gillian.'

He suddenly held out his hand and Gillian took it. He had a firm, strong grasp. She liked that in a man.

'And how do you feel about me?' he asked. 'Or are you disinclined to make snap judgements?'

Gillian grimaced.

'Considering how Stephanie took me in, I don't really know how to answer that question,' she admitted.

'Stephanie's a unique person,' David said. 'She took me in, too, and all the people she met, the friends we went to Stratford with. She was always so confident, so sure of herself. She never once tripped herself up or contradicted herself, but underneath she's frightened and lonely.'

'I suppose she told you her family, especially her older brother, are inclined to brow beat her?' Gillian said.

116

David looked surprised.

'No, she never said anything like that. I got the impression she loves her parents very much and adores Owen. I know you're engaged to him, Gillian.'

Self-consciously Gillian fingered her engagement ring.

'How does Stephanie really feel about that?' she queried in a hesitant voice.

'She's delighted. She speaks very highly of you, too.'

Gillian felt confused. All these facets to Stephanie's nature were disconcerting to say the least. David saw her hesitation.

'I don't say Stephanie doesn't have problems,' he said. 'She obviously has. When and how those problems started isn't easy to define, but I love her very much, Gillian, and I'm convinced I can help her if I'm patient and kind. And I think I can get her to come back here, but she needs to be assured, as I do, that doing so will be the best thing for her.'

'You need have no worries on my behalf,' Gillian promised him.

'But you're not sure about Owen or his parents?' David asked as though reading her thoughts.

'I'm sure they love her every bit as much as you do, David.'

David started to speak but was interrupted by Owen's sudden arrival. He strode in through the front door and through the open door of the sitting-room.

'Oh,' he said, when he saw David, who had quickly risen. 'I wondered whose the red car was.'

'Yes, it's mine.'

David held his hand out.

'David Sanderson,' he said, not waiting for Gillian to make an introduction.

'Owen Palmer.'

Owen shook hands, but there was a questioning look in his eyes.

'Stephanie's friend, Owen, you know, I told you about him,' Gillian said.

'Oh, yes, of course. I suppose you know where my sister is.'

Owen's tone was curt, but immediately David proceeded to repeat what he had already told Gillian. When he had finished Owen's grim expression had not lightened any.

'Stephanie has led us all a merry dance,' he said, 'and driven my parents half mad with worry. They just live from day to day, waiting to hear something.'

'Yes, I know,' David agreed placidly, 'but if you want her back you're going to have to forgive and forget. Do you want her back?'

'Of course we do.'

'Then I'll tell her that.'

'So you're to be the go-between, are you?' Owen threw at him.

David smiled.

'So it would seem.'

For the first time, Owen seemed to relax.

'Well, I must say if you're willing to take Stephanie on and marry her some day, I admire your courage.'

At that David laughed outright.

'I'm not afraid.'

He paused, looking intently at Owen whilst Gillian sat there saying nothing.

'So you won't stand in my way?'

'If you mean will I come over heavy handed about your marrying Stephanie, well, I shan't say, "Over my dead body", because Stephanie doesn't legally need anyone's permission to marry, least of all mine, but I'd ask you to wait, perhaps for a long time. Are you willing to accept that condition?'

'Any conditions you care to impose, Owen,' David said.

Once again the two men shook hands and at last Gillian felt it was the right moment to offer some refreshment.

'Tea? Coffee, anyone?' she asked.

'Coffee, please,' David said.

'Me, too, darling,' Owen put in.

As Gillian prepared the coffee in the kitchen, she could hear David and Owen chatting, their voices pleasant and friendly. They had taken to one another, she could see that, and she was glad. Perhaps the first hurdle had already been passed. Now, all that remained was to get Stephanie to come back here and then contact the Palmers in

Helmsley.

Obviously they would be very relieved that Stephanie was safe and well, but when they heard the full story? Well, Gillian was going to keep her fingers crossed because she had taken a liking to David Sanderson as well. He was only a few years older than Stephanie, obviously loved her very much and had only her long-term interests at heart. How could the Palmers possibly object to him?

When she took the coffee back into the sitting-room, Owen said, 'Gillian, you'll never guess what David does for a living.'

'Tell me,' she asked as she put the tray down on a table.

'He's an antique dealer, like me. What a coincidence.'

'That's right,' David said, accepting a cup of coffee from Gillian. 'I have a shop in Fairford.'

'Fairford?' Gillian gasped. 'Is that where you live, too?'

David smiled.

'Yes, it is. So now you know where Stephanie is, are you going to make a desperate, dramatic bid to take her away from me?'

'I don't think so,' Owen remarked. 'Do you think she'll agree to come back now?'

David shrugged.

'Well, I can but try. She's very scared, Owen.'

'Please,' Owen begged, 'tell her she has no

need to be scared.'

'I certainly will,' David promised.

After David had gone, Owen said, 'Well, I like the fellow. Perhaps he's the best thing that could have happened to Stephanie.'

Gillian went and leaned against him and he put his arm around her shoulders.

'Looks like there'll be a happy ending for all concerned,' she said.

'Well, I still have to ring home, you know.'

Gillian shot Owen a glance.

'Do you think there'll be a problem there?' she asked.

'Not if they've any sense there won't.'

'Do you think it might be better to wait till Stephanie gets here and see if she wants to speak to your parents herself?'

Owen considered this.

'Perhaps you're right. Yes, I'm sure you are. They've waited so long to hear from Stephanie that a little while longer won't hurt them. David said he'll try to get her to agree to come round here tonight. Do you know, Gillian, I'm the one who's scared, out of my wits.'

She kissed his cheek.

'Silly!' she teased gently, but she knew what he meant.

She herself felt trepidation at the thought of facing Stephanie again. They wouldn't simply be able to just kiss and make up, too much had happened for that. She decided she would just allow things to happen naturally.

They were watching the early-evening news when there was a ring of the doorbell. They both jumped up and Gillian switched off the television.

'I'll go,' Owen offered and quickly left the room.

Gillian could hear their voices in the hall, first David's, then Owen's then Stephanie's and she realised that Stephanie was crying. Gillian felt a rush of emotion and ran to the door. Owen was leading Stephanie inside, with David following on, looking very happy.

'Oh, Gillian,' Stephanie cried on sight of her.

Then they were in each other's arms.

'I'm so sorry for what I did, but I promise you, I promise you that I'll never do anything so wicked again. I've got David now and he's going to make sure I behave myself.'

She turned to smile at him. David pretended to be shocked.

'Hey, just a minute, don't make me out to be some sort of ogre,' he protested.

They all went into the sitting-room where David and Stephanie sat next to each other on the couch, holding hands. Tears still shone in Stephanie's eyes but she looked as happy as David did.

'I want to stay down here to be close to David,' Stephanie said. 'Can I stay here with you, Gillian?'

'Of course,' Gillian said at once 'for as long

as you like.'

'But remember, Stephanie,' Owen broke in, 'when Gillian and I get married we'll not necessarily be living here in Bourton.'

'Won't we?' Gillian was surprised. 'I thought we would.'

'So I've to sell up in Helmsley and move back here again, have I? May I remind you, darling, that my shop has been sold here and doing very nicely, thank you, in the capable hands of my successor?'

Gillian's face fell.

'Oh, I hadn't thought of that.'

Stephanie looked from one to the other of them.

'Am I being a nuisance already?'

'Don't be silly,' Gillian assured her. 'We'll work something out. Everything's negotiable, isn't it, Owen?'

Owen looked helpless but Gillian could see he wasn't cross. He glanced at David.

'You see what will happen if you get hooked up with this family, don't you, David?'

'I'm beginning to,' David confessed.

'We won't be getting married for ages yet,' Stephanie declared. 'I have to sort myself out first. I have to prove I can behave rationally and not be a worry to people. No, don't protest, Owen. I know what I've been like and I want to say this once and for all. I'm going to be different. I'm going to grow up.'

She stood up suddenly.

'And for starters I need to ring Mummy and Daddy. May I use your phone, Gillian?'

As the phone was in the sitting-room they all withdrew to the kitchen so Stephanie could make that vital telephone call in private. She was on the phone for what seemed ages. Gillian, David and Owen sat around the kitchen table.

'Have you two set a date yet?' David asked.

'Not yet,' they answered together.

'Soon,' Owen promised.

Gillian took hold of his hand across the table.

'Everything I went through seems like a fading nightmare,' she said softly.

'It was a nightmare,' Owen assured her, 'for all of us, but it's over. Spring's on its way and I don't think there'll be any more snow this year. And when we do have snow in the future, young woman,' he said and looked at Gillian with mock severity, 'I'm not letting you out of my sight.'

David and Gillian laughed then saw Stephanie had come in and was in the doorway.

'Well, that's that,' she said with a huge sigh of relief.

'Was it awful, Steph?' Owen asked in a kind voice.

Stephanie took the chair next to David who immediately put his arm around her shoulders.

'Well, Mummy cried and Daddy said he

wanted to strangle me, but at least they listened to me. I told them everything that had happened and they're coming down at the weekend. They want you to book them into a nice hotel, Owen, and Mummy seems to think whilst they're here it might be a good idea to have the wedding. Yours and Gillian's, I mean. Save another trip down here after. Will it be too much of a rush for you?'

She looked concerned.

'The sooner the better,' Owen said stoutly. 'We'll go and see the vicar tomorrow, and I suppose I'd better start looking round for another shop. Not too near Bourton, of course. I don't want to tread on Ian Westbury's toes.'

'Darling!' Gillian cried, her eyes lighting up with happiness.

'And may I be bridesmaid, Gillian?' Stephanie asked diffidently. 'That's if you don't mind.'

Of course she didn't mind. Gillian looked around the table. This was her family; these were her friends. Soon she would be Owen's wife, and in time, all being well, Stephanie herself would marry David. How could she ever ask for anything more?

We hope you have enjoyed this Large Print book. Other Chivers Press or G.K. Hall & Co. Large Print books are available at your library or directly from the publishers.

For more information about current and forthcoming titles, please call or write, without obligation, to:

Chivers Press Limited
Windsor Bridge Road
Bath BA2 3AX
England
Tel. (01225) 335336

OR

G.K. Hall & Co.
295 Kennedy Memorial Drive
Waterville
Maine 04901
USA

All our Large Print titles are designed for easy reading, and all our books are made to last.